Author Name: Lauren Wilson

ISBN: 978-1-957837-13-0

Published by: Excel Book Writing

Afro-Bougie Blues

Written By: Lauren Wilson

This short story collection is dedicated to my husband, Howard L. Wilson, Jr., for his enduring faith in me, in all things, in all ways

Contents

Mourning Angela

My body tried to warn me, but I didn't want to listen. So, it sent a back pain. I ignored it. A stomachache. Not feelin' it. The spotting was the final hint, and then the geyser came. Another miscarriage was dashing my hopes for motherhood.

It was 10 o'clock in the morning and I was midway through an experiment in the laboratory that would just have to wait until I could get back to it. My mind had flipped into mushroom mode, and all I could think of was getting back home to the comfort of my own bathroom, where I could hide from the world and cry in peace.

The drive home was mercifully brief and required enough concentration to block out everything but the pain. But when I got home, there was no more escape from the voices in my head. It was my fifth miscarriage in two years, and each one took another piece of my sanity and yanked it from my psyche. Alexis the Perfectionist couldn't do the most natural thing in the world. The rows of prenatal vitamins, immunological and Progesterone boosters, and herbal remedies mocked me from my medicine cabinet. I couldn't hide from the reality of my failure and the treachery of my uterus. Seventeen years ago, when I hadn't wanted to be pregnant, I was. Now at age 34, when I wanted to get pregnant, I couldn't. So, there I sat in my cream-colored bathroom, crying. Again. Just as I had five months ago and three months before that. I was sure this was some sort of punishment visited upon me by a vengeful God over the innocent life I had taken in my youth. My past had come back to haunt me; seventeen years ago, I had aborted a child.

Only my mother and my husband Terrence knew. To the rest of the world, I was a perfectionist ice queen who had probably never thought about love or sex for that matter. Instead, I had spent seventeen years immersed in books and research, clawing my way through college and grad school, then letting my Ph.D. and my "I'm in Control" attitude open new doors for me and slam shut on the disaster of my youth and my ill-fated attempt at love.

My marriage to Terrence had shocked my co-workers, but he had broken through my ice shield with an overwhelming barrage of warmth and laughter, pulling me out of my career-minded rut and giving me a reason to try to love again.

We had met when my lab needed an IT consultant to create a system for the reams of data that threatened to drown us. Terrence was completely in his element, sweeping in, learning everyone's jobs, designing a database that would fit who we were as scientists, and giving it enough bells and whistles to make us want to use it. All that with a laid-back "I Got This" attitude that was so different from our pressure cooker environment. In fact, I found myself cooking up excuses to be around him, presumably to help him tweak the database. He knew how to make me laugh at myself. And I loved it. After his contract was over, we started dating.

I remembered the night I had told him I'd been pregnant before. I had orchestrated it as the crucial moment in our relationship that it was. We had not yet had sex, but since the attraction was there, I wanted to tell him early -I didn't want it to be a secret. So we met for dinner at a seafood restaurant; I picked a place we'd never been to before to symbolize exploring new territory. I told him just before the check came.

"Terrence, there's something I need to tell you, and it could change how you see me as a person, but it's important. I think you know how much I like you. I hope we'll become very close, but you also need to know how seriously I take birth control. I got pregnant when I was seventeen. I thought I was in love, and I didn't understand enough about sex. I didn't think that one time would do it. But it did. The only thing I did know was I didn't want to be a teenaged mother or waddle through my senior year pregnant."

I stopped there. I'd never told another man. I'd never wanted to get serious enough with anyone else to trust them with that one piece of information, or rather those three pieces: I'd had sex at age seventeen, gotten pregnant, and aborted the child. It wasn't that I was ashamed or had remorse. I simply knew too many people wouldn't understand where I was coming from back then. For me, the abortion had been a pragmatic decision. There had been no angst at all, but no one liked to hear that. I was supposed to have anguished about this for days and weeks, teetered on the fence with it, and contemplated keeping the child and raising it myself. I did none of that. Instead, I aborted the child within me and never looked back.

I was not prepared for Terrence's reaction. With an uncharacteristically serious look on his face, he reached across the table, took my hands in his, kissed them, and told me it didn't matter to him. "Our pasts are in the past." Terrence paid the check and walked me to my car. He said, "Call me when you get home." Not, "I'll call you..." The door stood open to possibilities.

The relationship turned serious after that as I allowed myself to fall in love again. This time, to a man who could be silly, crazy, and competent at the same time. A man who had liked me enough to break through my ice queen exterior and awaken my inner child.

About three months after our dinner conversation, Terrence presented me with a nice, big, gift-wrapped box of condoms. We used them up quite gleefully in a short period of time. So, he bought more. A year and a half later, we eloped, honeymooned in Aruba, and started the fun-filled task of making babies. We'd been trying ever since... and two years later, we were failing miserably.

Because Terrence knew about my first pregnancy, it had never occurred to either of us that we'd have any problems creating a child. But after the second miscarriage, we went to a specialist to see if anything was wrong. We both checked out fine, so I started researching miscarriages and ways to prevent them. I followed every instruction and tried every remedy. The miscarriages kept happening. But this was the one that crushed me.

All of the other pregnancies had ended within a month, so when we got into the second month, complete with morning sickness and too-tight jeans, I'd gotten cocky. Terrence and I had fun trying the Old Wives' Tale of dangling my wedding ring over my belly. We knew we'd made a boy when it moved in a circle. I'd even peeked in the maternity section at Macy's. Their pants looked as though they were made for women who were in the third trimester, so I figured I'd just have to wear something elastic. Yes, that's how far it had gotten. But no, it was not meant to be.

Terrence came home early when he couldn't reach me at work. I'd already been in the bathroom for 5 hours, sobbing off and on and bleeding non-stop. I didn't want to come out, so he talked to me as I sat on the throne, saying anything he could think of that might comfort me but not really having the words. Finally, after he brought me hot herbal tea and Aleve, he started to talk about God. He told me that he prayed for my happiness more than he prayed for a baby - that a baby would come when God was ready to send us one. Sadly, I wasn't convinced and cried some more.

After two more hours, the worst of it was over. The Aleve had finally kicked in, so I left the bathroom, grabbed a diaper from the linen closet - after the first two miscarriages, I knew the routine - filled a hot water bottle, and climbed into the bed. Terrence lay down with me and rocked me back and forth until I fell asleep in his arms.

The dream started with gentle fluffiness. Then scenery appeared - a yellow room with little bears on the walls in red jackets. The curtains with little piglets and stuffed sad donkeys fluttered in an open window; a lamp with little balloons sat on a bureau in the corner; a cherry-stained wooden crib with yellow blankets and a mobile over top rested against the wall, along with a matching changing table. I was sitting in a rocking chair, barefoot with carpet under my feet, holding a baby. Nursing a baby. So contentedly. Stroking his fuzzy hair, smiling at his chubby little hands, ignoring the slight pain. Then my son let go of my nipple, with white dribble running down the side of his mouth, and looked up at me. He had the softest brown eyes with jet black eyelashes, a button of a nose, and plump cheeks, just like Terrence's baby pictures.

As he smiled at me, he began to fade. His beautiful brown skin became translucent as though I was looking through him at my lap. Then my baby disappeared altogether, and I sat there, bare-breasted, confused, shaken, and wondering where he went. I looked around, and the bears, piglets, and donkeys all looked back at me with sad eyes. The donkeys were crying. The balloons at the lamp base had turned into yellow roses for death and funerals. At that point, I knew my son was gone for good, never coming back. I began to cry.

As I rocked back and forth, sobbing in my chair, another image began to appear in front of me, a teenage girl, a carbon copy of me at seventeen. She had my long legs, curvy hips, rounded chest, and freshly permed hair. Then all of a sudden, she didn't look like me at all. She looked like a female version of Darryl, the boy who had gotten me pregnant seventeen years ago. He'd disappeared from my world as soon as I'd told him I had gotten pregnant. Deciding to abort little Angela - I thought of her as my angel - was even easier with him gone.

Darryl didn't love me the way he said he did when we'd been rutting like pigs in the back of his car. My mother hadn't understood why I'd named Angela at all. She thought naming the growing person inside of me would make it harder to get an abortion. But I believed Angela would understand, somehow. I was too young, too scared, too busy, too "teenage," self-centered, too carefree, just-plain-not-ready-to-be-a-mommy. Now Angela stood in front of me with a face that kept changing, sometimes looking like me, sometimes looking like Darryl.

I reached out to Angela, but my arms went straight through her body. Then she stepped toward me and through me; her memories, her thoughts, her feelings, her sensations became my own as we journeyed through her life.

Angela's abortion from inside me was an unpleasant sensation but muted from actual pain; the ability to sense pain was not there yet. But the ripping sensation of her soul leaving the flesh I'd created was unforgettable. Then, almost at once, we settled inside a new womb, one where we could grow healthy and strong. Angela came into the world with a different face, but she was still my daughter. The birth was a frightening experience; the horrible squeezing sensation, the air's frigid embrace, the desperate need to inhale. Then we were enveloped in a mother's arms and pecked on the forehead by a father beholding his first child. All of the pain had been worthwhile. Our emotions changed awkwardly as Angela's sisters came into the world, and Angela went from only to oldest. We longed for her parents' attention as she grew. We made efforts to be noticed and even stifled our shyness so we could bear the ballet recitals her mother inflicted on us - along with pain-filled toes and the overstretched muscles and other changes ballet created in our body. The first bicycle ride seemed as incredible as flying might be, feeling the flowing air, balancing with the grace learned in ballet, and conquering inner fears in order to go out into the world. There were a few scrapes and bruises from bicycle spills, but they were nothing compared with the wonderful sensation of the wind.

Time flew as we strove to master each school subject and earn each A that got Angela's parents' attention. Breasts grew, and menses flowed with the agonizing monthly pain. We discovered boys but kept our thoughts private - we were shy. We longed to be noticed and flinched at rejection when Angela's male classmates dismissed us as too brainy. Then time slowed with the conflicted emotions and new, unexpected sensations from our first kiss, stolen from behind a school building at the late age of seventeen. Overwhelming joy filled us as we raced off on our bicycle, heading home to journal that first kiss. Then the truck slammed into our body as we ran the red light, the wheels crushing the bicycle into our thigh, the broken ribs piercing through lungs and flesh. Then it was all over as our brain bounced and splattered on the roadway, and we could no longer feel the excruciating pain.

As I screamed, I could hear her saying: "Feel my death now so that you will appreciate your children."

Terrence heard the screams I had carried into my own state of awakeness. He held me as my body trembled, and my tears ran down below my ears and onto the pillow. I lay fetal and stayed that way until morning, reliving the feelings of this child who was my own but not my own, knowing I was finally mourning the death I hadn't mourned seventeen years ago.

When the morning did come, I had stopped shaking, although parts of me were still reacting to the realness of the dream and the feeling of crushing bones and hemorrhaging organs. As Terrence went off to work, I called in sick and then went to the front door in search of a newspaper out of some morbid sense of curiosity.

The obituary was on page three of the Metro section. Seraphina Robinson, age seventeen, had been killed in a truck accident while riding her bicycle. I wondered if I should go to the funeral. What could I say to this mother who did not know me and would not understand that this was also my daughter who had died? How could I tell her our daughter had known joy in the moments before she died, had savored her first kiss, had fallen in love? I realized my words could never comfort her, so I decided not to go.

###

For the next six months, I used a diaphragm while I sorted out my feelings about motherhood and the sanctity of life. When I was finally ready to try again, we conceived quickly, and as I hoped I would, I carried the pregnancy to term. We named our son Gabriel, my second angel.

Waking Dad

When Wesley Thompson refused to eat a Snicker's bar, Sharon knew he was truly dying. Her dad had never in her recollection turned down chocolate, and certainly not the luscious combination of chocolate, caramel, and peanuts. But by that time, everything else was gone, so it kind of made sense. He had had so many strokes Sharon had lost count. He'd lost his card sense, and Wesley Thompson could memorize 52 cards and 13 books as easily as adding two plus two. Wesley Thompson could add a stack of 6-digit numbers in his head back before calculators. It was a sad day when he couldn't add two plus two, and Sharon put the cards away. In the final days, he had lost his ability to speak, but not his ability to communicate. Like the time he dropped his drawers and stood in the doorway of the house just to let Sharon know that he was tired of kale and sausage soup. Sharon switched to Campbell's, and everything was honkey dory after that. But it was the Snickers bars that told her that it was time to call the family.

The next morning, Wesley's eldest daughter Lenore drove down from DC to North Carolina with her youngest daughter Aaliyah, who wanted to see her grandfather one last time. The middle daughter, Paulette, had flown in from Alabama a few days before; she and Sharon stood at their father's bedside, singing spirituals - at least the few they actually knew - just to be doing something that spoke of their love. Their dad hummed along; he wasn't gone yet.

But folks say Wesley Thompson died on purpose at the point when Lenore hit 90 miles an hour. The lights in the house flickered as his ghost flew up the highway to watch for cop cars and freak motorists who might stray in Lenore's path. She got there an hour too late to find her two younger sisters waiting for her, with the shell of her father in repose.

Wesley had moved into Sharon's house to die. The fight against cancer had been lost; in fact, the fight had gone out of him, and so she had opened her doors to her father to make sure his last days were spent surrounded by love. She supplied countless Snickers bars and Taco Bell chalupas, another of his favorite foods. Divorced dads don't always eat healthily.

Three daughters gathered together to say a last farewell. Their dad had secreted an ancient bottle of whiskey in the closet, and they opened it up, grabbed some paper cups from the kitchen, and filled them to the rim. And then the wake began.

"When I was young, I wondered if Dad had ever passed for white. Mom said he'd had red hair and green eyes when he was young, so I asked him one day. He said that he had tried it once.

Back in 1932, when he was ten years old, he snuck into a whites-only amusement park in DC. He hated it. What was so great about an amusement park that your friends couldn't go to? Why would anyone want to go on rides alone? He never did it again." Sharon told her story, gulped down a mouthful of whiskey, and passed the baton.

"Dad's great grandfather had been a slave, but Dad never really understood that. He just knew that his great-grandfather was a kind old man who wouldn't tell on him if Dad stole his cane. It was a game they played back when he was 5 years old." That was Lenore's piece.

"I remember when Dad took us to Aunt Jillian's third or fourth wedding. One of my cousins was playing with a baby. I asked if it was her brother, but my cousin said that this was her son. I didn't know that 14-year-olds could have children. But when I asked Mom later, she said it wasn't something she could explain just then." Paulette felt the burn of the whiskey on her lips.

"Grandpa used to babysit Makeda and me when Mom had an emergency at work. He taught us how to play spades, how to count cards, and how to make a bridge to shuffle with. We played with chips; he told us that if we played with pennies, that made it an entirely different game, and you had to take it seriously." Aaliyah wasn't but fourteen, but they let her have a sip from Lenore's cup.

"Do you remember when Star Trek came out? I was only 3 years old, but Dad loved it. He loved everything science fiction. He had heard HG Wells's War of the Worlds when it was broadcast on radio and talked about how it scared everyone - everyone thought that Martians had really landed on Earth. Dad loved Isaac Asimov and started me reading sci-fi books by the time I was 8." Another swig by Sharon.

"Dad had the neatest job. He let us go to work with him, and there were big banks of computers, and everyone had stacks and stacks of punch cards, each with one little line of information and tons of patterned holes. Sometimes he would let us feed the cards into the computer, and it would print out a calendar with a picture made of dots and dashes. The pictures were always shaped like naked women, but we just thought it was interesting that you could make a picture that way. He had his own desk, and one of the drawers had this secret stash of food. Peanut butter and crackers, mostly. And snickers bars." Pass.

"Dad wasn't old enough to fight until World War II was nearly over. But he enlisted anyway. Aunt Hannah has pictures of him in his uniform. I loved looking at them. It seems so strange to know someone who was part of World War II, but then, with colored regiments, most of them never saw combat. Cooks, drivers, mechanics. Unloading supplies and digging dishes. White people didn't want us showing that we could fight." Lenore again.

"Do you remember how Dad used to wake us up at 4 o'clock in the morning and drive us down to his favorite creek to go crabbing? I was always so scared that a crab was going to bite my toes, but he was fearless. He would pick one up with one hand, thumb and pinky across the crab body and throw it in his tin pail. Crabs in a barrel is so real. They would literally fight each other. Limbs came off. It was actually kinda gross, but they tasted good." Paulette was slurring her words a bit from the whiskey.

"I remember how much Dad loved to pass books around. I remember when he discovered Watership Down. He loved it so much that he got every one of us to read it. Do you remember that passage about when Hazelrah dies? I think I want to read it at Dad's funeral." Sharon got the hiccups.

"I'll never forget Thanksgiving dinners when the grown folks would gather in the basement to play bridge. Dad would let me sit on his lap and play the cards after he bid. If I did well, he would swell with pride. If I messed up, there would be a stern lecture. He took cards so seriously. I swear there must have been twenty bridge trophies on his bureau." Paulette shared one more memory.

Everyone was good and drunk by then. It was time to call the coroner.

"So, what should we do?"

"Cremate him." said Lenore. "I think that's what he wanted."

"What he wanted,"said Sharon, "was for us to put him in a boat in the middle of the Arctic Ocean and let the elements claim him once he got too feeble to be of any use to anyone."

"He may have said that 10 years ago, but that was before he started dying. Dad hung on to life at the end."

"Yes," said Paulette, "He did."

"Do you think they'll burn him in his clothes?"

"We can ask."

There was an old tuxedo in the closet. Sharon and Paulette lifted the body while Lenore worked each tuxedo arm and leg on. They had been talking for so long that the corpse had gotten stiff. But it was important that he have pants on.

"If they're going to burn him with his clothes on, then we should pack them with things that belong with him." Sharon rummaged around in his chest of drawers and found a deck of cards. Those went into one pocket.

"We need a Snickers bar. I'll run up to the store." The procured bar was stuffed into the other pocket. A handkerchief with his initials went into the breast pocket, and then Wesley Thompson was ready to meet his maker.

The coroners came with a gurney. With graceless practice, they flipped his body from the bed to the gurney. And then they wheeled him away. It made his death so final. When the daughters had been drinking, Wesley Thompson seemed present, but now, there was nothing but a corpse.

"We should do something more." thought Paulette.

"What do you have in mind?"

"Well, he still has some fireworks left," Lenore remembered putting them away when she had helped her dad move in with Sharon.

"It's May. Tell me you're kidding." Sharon thought about her neighbors.

"Nope," said Lenore. "Let's shoot off some fireworks."

They waited until it was dark out and then went out and stood on Sharon's back porch. The top of the package had sparklers; everyone lit up, and they swirled and twirled on the porch for a few minutes before getting down to the good stuff.

"Does anyone know how to do this?"

"Not really. I just know that you stand back."

In the end, the sisters decided to let Aaliyah light the first firework. She positioned a Roman Candle in the ground, lit it, and jumped back onto the porch. It sputtered for a few seconds, then went off in the air, spun around, and headed back to the house, hitting a window and bouncing off.

"Hmm. Too much wind."

She moved the next one further out. It was a starburst, and it lit up the sky above the house. It went on that way for a while. Lighting one, watching it erupt into color, then die down into sparkles. Then on to the next one. As a finale, everyone went out into the yard and lit four at once. Three daughters and a granddaughter saying goodbye. The night sky bloomed with light for a few moments and then faded to black, signifying the shortness of life within the grand scheme of things.

"Is that all?" asked Aaliyah.

"That's all. When it's over, it's really over."

Her Question

"Dad, I need to ask you a question." Aisha stood in the doorway of the den, decked out in a purple t-shirt and matching pajama bottoms, wondering if her father had heard her.

Unfortunately, Derek's attention was elsewhere. The Pittsburgh Steelers were up 3 points against the Baltimore Ravens, and Derek's eyes were glued to the TV screen. As the only Steelers fan at his office, Derek had bet $50 against the Ravens, giving the game added importance. In the back of his mind, Derek realized this might be The Question - the million-dollar question about boys he had dreaded since the day Aisha's mother had left three years ago. Aisha had been ten, and he'd had three years to think of an answer. He was still unprepared, and he wanted to watch the game.

"If the question is about boys, the answer is simple: leave them alone. If it's any more complicated than that, we can talk after the game."

The Ravens scored a touchdown but miraculously missed the field goal. Thirteen to ten, Ravens; Derek's money was running the wrong way down the field. He cradled the remote like a pacifier and grabbed a handful of Fritos from a table on the side of the recliner.

"It's kinda serious, dad."

Derek began thinking about Aisha. She had stopped wearing cornrows when her mother left, and now she had a thick, long ponytail. She had developed huge breasts two years ago, and he'd had his sister Janet take her bra shopping. This year, Aisha had started her period, and he'd added Kotex to the monthly shopping list. She had even started buying make-up with her allowance, hoping to mask the acne that had bloomed on her soft brown face. Janet swore that allowing a 13-year-old girl to wear make-up was a sign of weakness on his part, but Derek allowed it, deciding instead to put his foot down on low-cut tops and booty shorts. Luckily, those fashion statements weren't as big of an issue in autumn. Maybe thirteen wasn't too early for The Question.

"Is it about homework?"

There was a flag on the play, and the Steelers gained first down after a lousy pass. It was 3rd quarter, and anything could happen. Derek hoped it was a homework question.

"No, dad. It's okay; I'll go talk to Jada." Aisha bounded up the stairs to her room.

Sirens went off in Derek's brain. Jada was a provocative little ho-to-be. She wore heels that made her booty sway the way a 13-year-old's booty didn't need to be swaying. Her breasts exploded out of her shirts - not that they were buttoned to the top anyway. Jada wasn't someone Aisha needed to discuss The Question with. At the first commercial break, Derek dropped the remote in the recliner and sprinted up the stairs.

Aisha was hunched over on the side of her bed, talking on the phone, but it sounded as though she was talking to a boy. Derek stood in the doorway, looking at the juxtaposition of little-girl-purple-painted furniture with posters of hip-hop artists scattered all over the walls. He moved over to the bed as she got off the phone. She had a whipped dog look on her face and slumped shoulders. Not a good sign.

"OK, Aisha, what's the question?"

"Do boys fall in love the way girls do?"

Aisha had asked *The* Question. There went the football game. Nor had she asked the question he'd expected. He could have talked about the mechanics of sex or birth control. He could have told her all men lie to get sex. He had done it plenty of times himself, so he knew. But he also remembered the first time he fell in love.

He had been 15 years old, gangly, with a changing voice. As awkward an adolescent as Aisha was now, if he could have hidden in a closet that year, he would have. He had just begun his first year in high school, and he had joined the school band. His parents had talked him into playing the bassoon. He didn't even notice Yvette was interested in him until the fourth time she asked if they could practice together. She played the flute.

Yvette towered over most of her class. She had chestnut brown skin, her hair was pressed, and she wore it in a ponytail. She also had skinny legs and no chest. Nobody would have looked at her twice, including Derek, but she was 2nd chair, which meant she was very good at the flute. Derek knew playing with her would guarantee an A in Band, so they started practicing together. Derek thought of her as a friend - a good friend.

Junior prom came, and Yvette asked Derek to take her. His mother got him a tux and drove him to pick up Yvette on prom night. She looked nice. She'd put her hair up, and her dress showed off some unexpected curves. He had to admit she had serious booty; he'd never noticed before. At the prom, Yvette did not cling to Derek, and he appreciated it. They hung out with other kids from Band, danced during fast songs, and got cokes during slow songs.

At some point, Yvette and several other girls headed off to the bathroom, and Derek's best friend Darnell came up to him. "Yvette looks pretty hot. Have you ever had any of that?"

Derek had never given it any thought, but all of a sudden, his sense of honor kicked in.

"She's not like that. We're not like that. We're just friends."

"So, do you mind if I try to tap that?"

Derek realized he minded a lot. More than a lot. "I said she's not like that. Leave her alone."

"Okay, man. She's all yours. There are other hos to hit on." Darnell moved off.

Derek hadn't meant to stake a claim on Yvette. He just knew he wanted to protect her from dogs like Darnell. A slow song came on, and Derek took Yvette onto the floor, their hands on each other's shoulders, turning slowly so that they could look at everyone else.

"I didn't know Chris was going out with Deirdre."

"Yeah, they've been together for a while."

They watched as Darnell took a girl from the band onto the floor. He and the girl began to grind in slow motion as Darnell sucked on her neck. "I didn't know Darnell was into Joanne like that."

"He's not. He asked about you earlier."

"What did you say?" Yvette's tone held an odd curiosity.

"I told him you're not like Joanne."

"Anything else?"

"No. I just didn't think you needed everyone talking about you the way everybody's going to be talking about Joanne on Monday."

"No, you're right. I wouldn't want that." Derek thought he heard Yvette sigh.

The song ended, and the lights came up. Derek and Yvette walked down the school parking lot, looking for his mother's car. Yvette scooted into the back seat, and Derek climbed in after her. When they got to Yvette's house, she leaned over and kissed Derek on the cheek before she got out of the car. His blood rose in strange places, and he was embarrassed, but the moment passed.

"Thanks for taking me to the prom, Derek. I'll see you in Band on Monday."

Derek fell in love that night.

They had dated her senior year, but she broke up with him before she went to college. "You don't know it, but half the girls in Band stare when you walk by Derek, and people change in college. You need to have fun during your senior year." It hurt like hell. That day, Derek the dog was born, and sex had nothing to do with love for the next ten years... until he fell in love with Aisha's mother.

Answering Aisha's question would not be easy at all.

###

"Aisha, most times when a boy says he's in love, he doesn't mean it, but if you want, I can meet him, and then I'll be able to tell you for sure. What's his name?"

Aisha looked up. "His name is Jayson, and no, you can't meet him. You'd scare the crap out of him."

"OK, then let me give you a few clues. First of all, he won't ask you to have sex."

"Serious?"

"No, he won't." Derek shook his head." If he has, he doesn't love you."

"I don't believe you.?" Aisha pouted.

"OK, let me give you another clue. If he loves you, he'll want to meet me."

"What do you mean?"

"If he loved you, he'd want to know me because I'm a major part of your life."

"OK, tell me another one." Aisha looked up again, and Derek could tell he had her attention.

"Has he told you you're his girlfriend?"

"Yes."

"Have you met his mom yet?"

"Yes, she comes to some of his games. He told her we were friends."

"Jayson doesn't love you, Aisha. If he loved you, he would have introduced you as his girlfriend."

"Oh." The whipped dog look came back, so Derek sat down and put his arms around her.

"Aisha, I didn't say he doesn't like you. He probably does, but love is something different. When guys fall in love, we get overprotective. We want everyone to know you're special to us, and we do special things for you, so you know. Oh, and we do NOT say 'I love you' as many times as you'd like us to because it's redundant. If a guy loves you, he'll show you instead of telling you."

"I don't want to believe you."

"Then let me play, dad, and say, you don't have to believe me. Just don't have sex with him. Can you do that much for me?"

"I don't know, Dad. I love him. I think he's the one."

"If you're not the one for him, then he's not the one for you. No matter how much you care for him, if he isn't doing the things I told you about, then he doesn't see you as the only one for him. Let's look at it another way. Do I come across as overprotective?"

"Seriously."

"That's because I love you. Do I introduce you to everyone as my daughter and then show off how proud I am of you?" Derek gave her a squeeze.

"Yes, and it's embarrassing." Aisha groaned.

"But I do that because I love you. Last question: am I trying to talk you out of having sex at age thirteen?"

"Yes, dad."

"It's because I love you. And right now, nobody out there loves you as much as I do. Don't get me wrong. I don't expect you to stay celibate forever. But there's a time and a place, and you're not there yet."

Aisha swiveled around in his arms. "Jada's already had sex."

That caught Derek off guard. He looked his daughter in the face. "Yeah, and Jada's a ho." His voice was harsher than he had meant it to be. "I'm sorry. I shouldn't call your friend a ho, but if she's telling you to have sex because she's having sex, then she's a lousy friend, and you need to dump her pronto."

"I can't just dump my best friend," Aisha whined.

"Then stand up to her and let her know you're not always going to do everything she does. Maybe you should let Jada hang out with you over here."

"Why?"

"I'll cook dinner."

"Dad, your cooking sucks," Aisha whined again.

"OK, I'll order pizza. Maybe if Jada sees what you and I have, she'll understand why you don't need to have sex. Maybe she won't see it, but I think it's worth a shot."

"Can she stay overnight?"

I'll talk to her mother."

"Jada's mother isn't like you. She won't care."

"Then Jada should see what it's like when a parent cares." Derek began to raise his voice again.

"Ease up, Dad." And Aisha groaned again.

"OK, I'll leave it alone, but don't do things because Jada tells you to. Be your own person.

"OK."

"And when you think you're at that time and place, we'll talk about condoms."

"No thanks, dad." Yet another groan.

"If you can't talk about condoms, then you are absolutely positively not ready to have sex. Has Jayson talked to you about condoms?"

"Gross."

"See, that's what I mean. If he wants sex but won't talk to you about condoms, then he doesn't love you."

"You've said that already."

"Sorry. Remember, I didn't say he doesn't like you. I'm sure he likes you, but you need to dial it down on the love thing."

"OK."

"I love you, Aisha."

"I know that."

"Can I go back to my game now?"

"Sure, dad. I'm going to call Jada."

The Ravens beat the Steelers 20 to 13. It would have hurt to watch, and some things were more important.

Fear of Falling

It seemed so cliché. There he was, making love to Candi Davidson, Mrs. Candi Davidson, when he felt pains in his chest. It was unfair. One was supposed to come, then go, not the other way around. But there was no helping it. Bryan Willis was having a heart attack in a sleazy motel room in the midst of a tryst with a married woman. As he lay there gasping and trying to say "Help," he could tell Candi thought he was just sated. He pointed to his heart, and she got the message. She called 911 as she got dressed and called the front desk seconds before she fled out the door. He couldn't blame her. It was not the best situation to be in. The paramedics came, and Bryan could feel the defibrillator but was beyond words. And then, he was beyond feeling, or rather, he was beyond feeling the defibrillator. What he did feel was a sense of falling. A horrible feeling. Bryan's worst fear was falling off a building or a cliff while looking down. He always stood ten feet away from all scenic views. He never stood at the edge of a boat. That was the extent of his fear, and now he was falling.

Life did not flash before his eyes; it rolled through his mind in slow motion. From Bryan's first recollections of his father: his admiration, his desire to be like him, to the fun he had with all of his half-siblings when his dad had his 50th birthday party. The mothers hung at the edges, watching their children but managing not to interact with each other, each knowing that at some point, they had held the favor of Cliff Willis. He remembered his mother saying "Damn the man" so often, but with an impatient sigh instead of real anger. He hoped a woman would say that about him someday. Maybe several women. Money was always tight, and he got his share of beatings for wanting more until he learned that other girls would line up to give him things. He knew he was good-looking. Buddies hung around him to pick up his cast-offs. Life was good.

Bryan had had three wives but eventually realized that marriage wasn't for him. He could never be faithful; he never wanted to be faithful. Each wife left him, and each wife asked for child support. None of them got any. Bryan never worked. He just lived with women, loved women, made love to women, and left women when they got needy. He was so like his father, his mother said. The highest praise.

He was still falling. He felt little whimpers escape from his lips, his arms flailed, and his legs kicked out. He tried to find purchase, tried to do anything to stop the horrible motion, the sensation of his worst nightmare.

He thought about his children, many of the same age all shapes and sizes as were his women. He loved children; he loved making children. He had a sense of pride that came with each time a woman came to him and said, "I'm pregnant, Bryan." It made him strut, hold his head up, and feel like a man. Even if he didn't work, even if he had no talent for the day-to-day grind, he could still sire children with the women in his life. So many children. Sometimes he was sorry he had no money for them, but most of the time, he wasn't. That was for the women to take care of. It was enough that he was proud of them.

And he was still falling. He began to attempt to reason, despite his panic. He had never known anyone to speak of falling as a near-death experience. They always talked about seeing a bright light or going through a tunnel. He had never heard of a sense of fear. Maybe there was a reason.

He had never given any real thought to God. It was something women did. They went to church, they sang, they spoke in tongues, they repented, they filed to the altar, they were filled with the Holy Spirit, and they gave up their Sundays. To Bryan, Sundays were for sleeping in, exhausted from the partying and loving that came the night before. His only memories of church were as a child, being dragged by the ear by his mother until he was old enough for her to get tired of dragging him. Maybe fourteen. Around the time he started having sex was the time he decided the Bible had gotten it all wrong. The world was a glorious place, and the other place, heaven, with singing angels, but no dancing, no sex, no curvaceous women, was not for him. Let him stay on earth as long as possible, and let the women worry about heaven. There was some talk of hell, but Bryan didn't believe in that either. Fire and brimstone, little red men with pointed horns, tails, and pitchforks. It was a fairy tale. Sure, he'd read Dante in school: The Inferno with levels of despair and agony. They were more fairy tales designed to scare people into being good. It didn't work on most men; hell, it didn't work on most women. He saw more hypocrisy among women than he had words for. They partied the night before and repented afterward. Hoping for heaven by denying oneself everything good in life, then "falling" from grace whenever something fun happened. He thought of a few of his guy friends who had "caught religion" as though it was a disease. One he stayed far away from.

He was still falling.

Bryan began to wonder. They said that hell is down below. What if I am going to hell? What if hell is real? Why would it be me? What did I ever do that was so wrong except to love women and bring some joy to their lives? Maybe it was time to catch religion. Maybe it was time to pray. Bryan wasn't sure how to do it, but he began to pray to the best of his ability. "God, I don't do this falling thing well. I'm surprised I haven't thrown up already. I'm starting to get a bit worried about things. God, are you hearing me?

Are you really all around? Are you really all-wise, all-knowing, all capable of changing situations? Because I'd like this situation to change, God."

Nothing happened.

"I was right. There is no God. No God would let something like this happen. I feel like I've been falling for hours, if not days. I see no bottom. I don't want to see a bottom because hitting the bottom is going to be horrifically painful. The bones of my face will get pushed into my brain. My limbs will shatter. My neck will snap. My penis will be crushed. Poor penis. And my balls are going to hurt like hell."

Like hell.

He was dying and going to hell.

Maybe he could say he was sorry. He remembered each divorce and the vindictiveness of his wives: the anger, the screaming, the throwing things. Should he have apologized for doing what came naturally? Should he have apologized for getting married? Sometimes, Bryan would meet a man and know he had slept with that man's wife. Should he have apologized and probably been punched out? Or apologize to the women for seducing them? Or for letting himself get seduced by them? It wasn't as if there weren't plenty of single women. Maybe he should have stuck with single women. Maybe he shouldn't have had so many children. How could that be right? Be fruitful and multiply. He had been exponential. But maybe he would have still been a man with fewer children. And maybe a job. Should he be sorry that he never held down a job? That he never sent money for sneakers, never took his children out?

But the worst possibility was that he was supposed to be sorry for not going to church. For not "getting saved." For not giving up what he loved most, or giving up some of it, and focusing on the things that might have made sense to him if he'd been more open to them. So many women went to church. Could it have been more important than he thought?

And God? Would this be happening if he had learned to pray?

He hit the ground. Hard. He felt the bones splinter, the organs burst. The weight of his tailbone crushing his testicles. It was worse than he imagined. And yet he was alive. Or was he dead? He couldn't tell anymore. No one should survive such a fall. He must be dead. He must be in hell. This was hell. To fall for what felt like an eternity, to feel crushed, ground into dust, and... no. The earth opened up, and he was falling again.

It was his worst nightmare. Endless falling. Endless terror, endless dying, endless pain. No one had told him. Maybe no one had known. He wished he could tell someone that this was what hell was like. And that being sorry meant nothing, calling out to God meant nothing, seeing any error in your ways meant nothing. He thought about Candi. Would she fall? Or would she scurry off to church and repent. Maybe she would be saved. He hoped so. No one deserved this. Or maybe some people did. Ax murderers, rapists, serial killers, suicide bombers. They deserved this. Had what he had done been so wrong?

Maybe it had. Maybe he had messed with people's lives. Maybe he wasn't a criminal, but what he had done still hurt people. Maybe hurting people was the sin that he was being punished for. That he could not say he was sorry soon enough.

Bryan thought these things as he fell. And he thought them over and over again, for eternity.

Confessions of an Adulteress

I fell in love with Jessie Barnes the first moment I heard her. Trust me; it wasn't from looking at her. My cousin was downright homely: plump, wore glasses, had rough brown skin, and little sense of style. But when I heard her speak, everything changed. Jessie had a way of drawing you in with a story, and when she started talking about history, it was fascinating. I was at a family reunion on my family's side with Mark and the twins. Marcy and Nidra were 6, and it was the first, and only reunion Mark ever agreed to go to. Mark and the twins had gone to bed early, so I snuck down to the lobby bar to hang out. Jessie was holding court, telling stories about our family history.

"Now, our great-great-grandfather ran away. He ran from Frankfort, Kentucky, to Ohio to Michigan and across Lake Erie to Ontario. His siblings got sold down to Nashville, while our great-great-great grandparents remained in Frankfort. It was the Freedman's Bureau that got the family back together after the Civil War, and Great Great Grandfather Jefferson came back from Canada. And now we're all here sitting around drinking at a bar that wouldn't have served us 80 years ago." I was fascinated. I'd never heard anyone talk about our history before. Heck, I'd never been interested in history. But this was about MY family. It actually had relevance. It was a turn-on. Meanwhile,

Jessie could sing, too. As everyone got drunker, Jessie started singing back-in-the-day songs from Minnie Ripperton, Deniece Williams, and even Sarah Vaughn. No backup. That did it. I had a crush on my cousin. As the crowd broke up, I went over and introduced myself. Jessie asked who my parents and grandparents were. That's when she established that we were fourth cousins, from the same town, on my father's side. Not that I knew my father well, which explained why we'd never met before. I'd never had a crush on a woman in my life. It felt naughty. Something meant to be a secret. But I hugged her. All that roundness actually felt good. And I discovered a side of myself that I'd never known.

You have to realize that I love men. Take my husband Mark, for example. Mark is, hands down, one of the most handsome men on the planet. Don't take my word for it. Ask any black woman and probably many white women in Frankfort. He's got smooth ebony skin, soft eyes, a strong chin, and chiseled cheeks; his biceps burst through his shirts, and when he's naked, you can count his pectorals. I'm not unattractive myself, but I know I got myself a prize. That old adage about playing hard to get surprised me with its effectiveness. We didn't even make love until after I had a 1-karat diamond on my finger - not bad for a college kid, even if he was a track star. Keeping Mark interested takes a lot of energy; he just doesn't know it. Even after I had the twins, I kept my college-slim figure. I make sure that I'm sexy when I come to bed if I can tell that he's in the mood. No cucumber face packs, flannel nightgowns, or pin-curled hair. If I want bouncy locks, I use a curling iron in the morning. Unbeknownst to my husband, I even study sex tapes so that when HE thinks of something new and innovative, I can flow with it. And we have an understanding. Mark was in a frat in college that did unspeakable things to insecure women. Even though he didn't do it himself, he didn't stop it. I knew that my husband was going to have affairs, so my rule was: no diseases, no drama. It's something we both can live with.

So, we have a good sex life, and I always thought I was as hetero as a woman could get – until Jessie.

I saw Jessie at family reunions over the next few years. I would get a teen-aged cousin to keep an eye on the twins while I'd sneak down to the bar on Saturday night. She was always telling her history stories, and I always gave her a hug at the end of the night. Once I gave her my signature shy smile, and I wondered if she knew about my crush, the way she smiled back.

Mark and I lived in Frankfort, where my greats had been slaves. Mark was a track coach at Kentucky State University and was on the road a lot during the season. I had a job there as a math lecturer and made sure that I only had early classes so that I could pick up the twins after school. As I met more of my father's relatives, one of my cousins introduced me to Ruth Baker, Jessie's mother, when she got a job teaching history at KSU. We hit it off instantly, and she became a big part of my world. I would take the kids over on weekends, and they would play in the backyard while we talked, enjoying how the conversations ranged from music to history to current events. Conversations with Mark weren't very deep and usually focused on sports. A discussion about Jim Crow in Frankfort would bore him to tears. Mark sat in on one evening with Cousin Ruth and complained about it the entire way home. "Doesn't that woman talk about anything but the past? Who wants to hear about slavery anyway? There's nothing to be gained from talking about it. She needs to step into the 21st century." I was actually relieved. I didn't want to share Cousin Ruth.

Three years after that first family reunion, Cousin Ruth told me that Jessie was moving to Frankfort to work for the KSU Music Department. She would teach voice and jazz history. I played semi-interested; I wasn't going to tell anyone about my crush. Jessie and her family of 4 ended up spending two crowded months living with her mother while she and her husband James looked for a house. James Barnes was so in love with his wife that it astounded me. To him, she was clearly the most beautiful, fascinating, sexy woman in his world. His head never turned, and I found myself wishing that Mark was like that.

When they turned nine, the twins announced jointly that they wanted ballet lessons. Mark was excited because it was a sign of athleticism that he was determined to cultivate. I was excited because everyone else was, though I secretly wondered how long their enthusiasm would last. I found a dance studio and trotted them off to ballet lessons on Wednesdays, spending my free time at the local library. Interestingly enough, Jessie enrolled her 7-year-old daughter Dana in the same class. We would have coffee at a small café near the library and talk for a half-hour until it was time for me to go get the twins. Our hugs had evolved into kisses on the cheek. And I would give her my shy smile. Two years later, when the twins grew tired of ballet - I hadn't thought it would hold their interest that long - we looked around for something else that might pique their interest year-round so that I could continue meeting Jessie for coffee. We knew that Dana would happily go wherever the twins went. She idolized them. I settled for karate, found another studio in an all-white part of town and another cafe where we could meet, and exchange a kiss and a hug at the end.

By the time we'd been having coffee together for two years, my crush had blossomed into something a bit more, shall we say, intimate. I would get a big grin on my face at the thought of seeing Jessie, and there was a tingle between my thighs whenever we got together. I wasn't prepared to question my sexuality, but I had to admit that I wasn't as straight as I thought I was. What shocked me was to find out that her feelings matched mine. I don't remember exactly when things started to change. We had been sitting at our regular cafe when Jessie reached across the table and began to caress my fingers. Her hand felt soft and warm, but this new intimacy wasn't something I was prepared for. I'd never told Jessie how I felt. Maybe it was written all over my face, but it never occurred to me that there would be reciprocation. I pulled back my hand and wished I hadn't. It was about 2 months later that I got up the courage to kick a shoe off and rub her leg. Her face crinkled into a slow, easy smile. I suggested that maybe we could spend a bit more time together. She said she would think about it. And we left it at that for a while. Sometime in the spring, we talked about what our schedules might look like the following semester, and we found a hole. We were both free after 1 pm on Fridays. The summer went by very slowly.

That very same school year, when the twins turned 14, I quietly nudged them toward Track. They were both tall and lanky like Mark and had developed stamina from karate. I was sure that Mark would be thrilled. The twins started staying late after school to train, getting home at 5 and 6 pm. I felt as though God was smiling down on me and letting me know that what I was going to do wasn't as bad as it seemed. Jessie's 16-year-old son Damon was pretty much on his own after school, and Dana was cheerleading in middle school, so she wasn't getting home until 4:30. Jessie found us a hotel near Lexington, a good 15 miles outside of Frankfort. We met at 2 pm in the afternoon, and the motel wasn't as empty as it should have been. There were other individuals quietly moving in and out of rooms, which were booked for an evening but only used for an hour. I chickened out, so Jessie sang to me for the next two hours until it was time for both of us to leave. But the following week, I'd shed my inhibitions, and we made love. Jessie sang to me as I undressed, and kissed my toes. The rest was actually indescribably beyond wonderful and better than anything Mark had ever done. And that was how we spent our Friday afternoons. It was glorious, and a part of me wondered why we'd waited so long.

At the same time, things at home were not so wonderful. The twins were hanging out with Mark a lot when they weren't training, and something must have happened because Marcy came to me one day and asked if Mark was having an affair. I didn't know what to say. I sat both of them down and let them cry for a while. I told them that it wasn't a reason to hate their father, especially if I was okay with it. They stopped hanging out with their father as much, and I thought that they would quit track altogether. So, I stopped my dalliance with Jessie so that they could have my Friday afternoons. We did girl stuff. Malls, pedicures, make-up sessions. We took a trip to Nashville one weekend just to go somewhere different. And eventually, things fell back into place. I think it was because they could see that it didn't bother me. And it didn't. Not because I was sleeping with Jessie, but because I knew that Mark loved me, and his affairs didn't change that. My affair didn't change that. But the intricacies of the games adults play are not to be foisted on one's children. Mark and I talked about his affair, and he responded heroically by making special father-daughter time with them and eventually re-won their hearts.

It was only when the twins were settled back into their routine with their father that I felt comfortable seeing Jessie again. We were making up for lost time, and I sense that we weren't sufficiently discreet. Cousin Ruth was the first one to catch on. She came by my office at the university at 1 pm on a Friday, closed the door, and sat down. "Somebody is going to see you, and it won't be pretty. You need to stop before it really gets out of hand."

I was so embarrassed. "How did you know?"

"I've always known about Jessie; I just didn't know about you."

You could have plopped an egg in my mouth; my jaw dropped so far. "So Jessie's bi?"

"Always has been. And James knows. He may not know about you, but he's always accepted the fact that Jessie goes both ways. But I don't think Mark would understand. At all."

"No, he wouldn't."

"I've seen the way you two look at each other lately. Eventually, someone is going to put two and two together, and it won't be pretty. End it."

"I don't know how."

"All good things must come to an end, Deidre. You have too much at stake. I'll talk to Jessie. Sometimes she just won't admit that the world isn't ready for people like her."

After that little talk, I told Jessie that I wanted to break it off. But we didn't. We just got together a bit less frequently, a bit more randomly. She would put a rubber band on the door of my office, and I would sneak off for a moment of joy.

Unfortunately, one of the twins was the second one to catch on. "Mom," said Nidra, "why do you always seem so happy on Fridays? Are you having an affair?"

If I'd been embarrassed in front of Cousin Ruth, I was mortified in front of Nidra. I didn't know what to say. I tried to play it off.

"It's the weekend, and I'm happy to be done with school."

She didn't leave it alone. "Mom, please be honest. I won't like it, but it's not like I would hate you if I don't hate dad."

"I do like someone. I guess you could say that I have a special friend who makes me happy. But I really don't want to discuss it."

"I won't tell, mom. I'm glad you're happy." And Nidra didn't tell Marcy for a long time because Marcy and I didn't have to have the talk until she was 17. She didn't take it as well.

"How could you? It's wrong. It's a sin. It's disgusting."

For a moment, I thought that Marcy realized that I was with another woman, but then I realized that any affair was a sin in her eyes. And I didn't have any comebacks. I sat her down; I hugged her. "I know it's all those things." I had to pause. I actually didn't know what to tell her. She was crying hysterically, and all I could think to do was rock her in my arms and say, "I'm sorry." Over and over again.

Because I really was sorry that I had hurt her. Just as Cousin Ruth had said – someone was going to get hurt. When the sobs slowed down to sniffles, I reached for a Kleenex and wiped her nose. And said nothing. There just wasn't anything to say.

At the same time that the twins started college, Jessie was given the opportunity to teach at Oberlin Conservatory in Northern Ohio. I knew she'd take it. You don't turn down a world-famous conservatory. But it hurt like hell. I sulked, I screamed, I cried. All in a small private hell of my own, away from Mark, away from Jessie, whom I was putting up a brave front for to keep from dulling her excitement. I decided to throw myself into my marriage. I cranked up the heat in the bedroom; I worked out, and I attended Mark's meets like a schoolgirl. And it backfired because Mark realized the truth.

"You've had an affair, haven't you?"

We were coming home from a black-tie affair that his fraternity had held, one of those events where being the perfect couple mattered, and we were dressed to fit the bill. He'd gotten a haircut; I'd had my hair and nails done, new dress, low cut – I could still pull it off, perfect make-up, perfect wife. Somehow it just made it worse.

"Whenever I had an affair, I always felt that I had to make it up to you. I'd be more tender, more attentive; I'd buy you presents." I knew all of that. I guess my duplicity was obvious.

I debated whether to tell him about Jessie. Would it make things better or worse? I wasn't sure, so I didn't risk it.

"It's over. For good. Never again." I said. And I knew it was true. Jessie would probably find someone else, and I didn't want anyone else.

"Who with?"

"Does it really matter? At any rate, I'd rather not say. We're both married." No dishonesty; I just couldn't reveal the truth.

"No, if it's over, I guess it doesn't really matter."

"It will never happen again, Mark. Truly."

"Deidre, don't make promises. I never made promises I couldn't keep."

"True," I said.

Mark, I still love you. I'm still in love with you. Please know that."

"I know. You want me to drop it, don't you?"

"Yes, very much."

"Do the girls know?"

I wanted to lie. They had kept my secret, as I had kept so many of theirs. Mark had never known how sexually active they were, that each of them was on the Pill, that there had been pregnancy scares. They were his precious babies. Innocent in his eyes.

"Yes, they know. I think they are more in tune with us than we realize. I never wanted to hurt anyone, Mark. It just happened."

"I'll get over it. Was he as handsome as I am?"

"No, definitely not."

"What did you see in him?"

"Just an interesting personality, I guess. You know what a sucker I am for that intellectual stuff."

"True. Well, we've had an intelligent, grown-up conversation about it. I hope you don't mind if I just drop you off at the house. I think I need a drink."

I wondered if he would go somewhere and get laid, but it really wasn't any of my business.

"I love you, Mark."

"I know, Deidre."

We kissed before I got out of the car. It was a slow kiss with longing. A make-up kiss. We had had many, but never one quite like this. I walked to the front door and waved as he left. I didn't see him again until the morning.

#####

About 5 years after Jessie and James had moved their family off to Ohio, we were at another family reunion when James came up to me quietly and invited me for a walk.

"I think you were good for her, Deidre."

I wasn't sure that I was prepared for this conversation, but as Cousin Ruth said, it wasn't as though he didn't know.

"It puts a certain passion in her singing. It takes her somewhere I can't go. Jessie is like a butterfly; trying to hold her would crush her, and it's the last thing I would ever want to do."

"You're a wonderful husband, James."

"Thanks for that, Deidre. Thanks a lot. I have no regrets."

Jessie sang at the bar that night, and James and I sat at a table together, soaking it in, enjoying the butterfly that Jessie would always be. She blew a kiss in our direction. James and I looked at each other and smiled.

Alone with My Nightmares

I only drink at night. I'm not sure why. All the death I saw happened in broad daylight. But I can hold off the memories during the day. Maybe it's because I keep busy. I did 4 tours in the Persian Gulf: one in Saudi Arabia, one in Turkey, one in Iraq, and one in Afghanistan. That's what you call a glutton for punishment, but I wanted my 20 years and a pension. I tell my wife that I was in the Quartermasters Corps, cooking for troops and managing supplies. It's an easy lie. She doesn't need to know what I really did. I'm not sure what she'd think.

I've killed people. And not from a distance; I've shot people in the face. Just to keep me or my unit from getting killed. As I said, I don't know why the flashbacks only come at night. I guess I'm lucky. They call me a functional alcoholic. I can get up in the morning, hungover but awake, and go to work every day. Sometimes it amazes me that I manage to get up in time for the 5 am shift, but it's probably because I start drinking early and pass out early. Nor do I always get drunk. I don't think my wife would have stayed with me if I did that. I'm not sure why she stays with me now. I think she takes her vows pretty seriously. More good luck on my part. We've been married for over twenty years now. And she knew me before I went over. I'm pretty sure that that's why she stays with me; because she knew me before.

I'd like to think that I was a decent husband before I went to the Persian Gulf. I drank socially, but I knew when to quit; I brought home enough money for us to be comfortable; I loved my kids as much as I loved making them. We'd moved from Baltimore to Fort Bragg, and I was cooking for new recruits and the Airborne Corps. Then it all changed. I remember when our battalion was called in 1989, and I said my goodbyes. It was my first time going overseas. It would be Tamara's first time being truly alone. I knew she was dreading it. The sex, of course, was awesome. It was going to have to tide me over for a year, and she made it quite memorable for an entire week. Somehow, I sensed that there would be a new kid on the block when I got home.

My first tour in the Persian Gulf was around the time of Operation Desert Storm. I say around the time because we were there a lot earlier than people remember. Officially, we were saving Kuwait. But why lie. We were saving one of our oil sources. Nobody pretended that it was glorious. We just knew that this was how we were going to serve our country, and we were going to do it well. I really was in the Quartermasters Corp as a cook back then. Most of the time, I had it easy. I was attached to an anchored regiment in Saudi Arabia that wasn't going anywhere. I got up, I cooked, I cooked some more, I cooked one last time, and then I fell out until the next day. Every once in a while, it got crazy. For some reason, maybe my tendency to say dumb things at the wrong time, I seemed to get attached to combat units with an alarming frequency. Jumping when they jumped, running when they ran, ducking when they ducked, scrambling when they scrambled. Not quite what I had signed up for, but I was "Supporting Victory" - the Quartermaster motto. And I was just a kid.

I had to kill someone on my very first tour. Even though Operation Desert Shield was supposed to be a border mission with little action, I saw some. I was part of a cavalcade that got ambushed. We had more ammo than they did, thank goodness. But it still meant that I was one of the soldiers who dealt out death. Even I, a lowly cook, was armed and dangerous. I put holes in human beings at the same time that they were trying to put holes in me. We were victorious if you could call it that. We left a lot of dead bodies behind, but we also took one of our own. It surprised me that the nightmares didn't start then and there. But there was too much to do. The Army is very structured. We all rise, we all eat, we all exercise, we all have a day's worth of assignments, we all take shifts at night, and we all try to get some sleep. We wake up the next day and do it again. I noticed that others had nightmares. I counted myself lucky. And I counted the days until I could go home.

As I suspected when I left, I came home to a 3-month-old daughter. Tamara named her Desiree for Desert Shield. There were a lot of 3-

month-old kids on base that year. It was a good thing. Lots of moms to bond with, lots of kids to play with. Too bad I didn't get to see it for very long. Two weeks after I got back from Saudi Arabia, I was in Turkey, defending the Kurds from the Iraqis. They called it Operation Provide Comfort. More like Provide Cover. There was a lot of action that nobody talked about.

When I got back to Fort Bragg, things were actually rather boring. I was cooking for the new recruits and the Airborne Corps. Cooking at a training facility is cushy, so I was on my best behavior. Next was Fort Leonard Wood in Missouri. I was going anywhere I could as long as I could stay in the service. I left Tamara and the kids with her parents in Baltimore when I went to Korea to Camp Market, just to bake. And then came Bush Jr. and Haliburton, and the writing was on the wall for cooks. I could see that civilians would be taking over, so I started thinking about what I could do next. Then 9/11 came, and the Axis of Evil and I knew we were headed back to the Persian Gulf. When I headed back to training school, I picked the one non-combat duty I couldn't see them outsourcing: Mortuary Affairs. You pick up the dead bodies, figure out who they really are, and make sure they get home, hopefully, without somebody trying to kill you. To tell the truth, it's about as combat as non-combat gets.

I was in Operation Iraqi Freedom when the nightmares started. I had thought I could handle it. I'd seen people get shot and killed; I figured it couldn't get much worse. I hadn't counted on suicide bombers. The next thing I knew, I was seeing parts of people, sometimes keeping them together, sometimes not. There was a man whose head was only partially severed from his neck. It lolled over to one side. Before, it had just been bodies riddled with ammunition. Now, it was very different. My dreams were like freakshows. I saw parts of people moving in front of me. Instead of the amputees that we were shipping home, I saw arms grasping, legs walking. Sometimes, I saw body parts reconnecting to the wrong body. They called it post-traumatic stress disorder. I just called it a damned good reason to drink.

So, I was already drinking when I got to Afghanistan. People don't remember that we've been there since 9/11. All they remember is Obama's brave talk about shifting the war. They also don't like to think about the body count. But it's pretty bad. The Taliban hate us, and it seems like they hate their own. They don't mind killing children Desiree's age – with homemade bombs that literally blow them to bits. I think it gives them a hard-on. That's why I don't mind so much when we kill them.

A lot of times, when we were picking up bodies, we'd come across somebody who was still alive. A head and a torso, but not much else. Maybe two arms, maybe not. Nobody talks about the wounded. From what I've seen, some of them might be better off dead.

I made my twenty years in 2009, right around the time that Obama got conned into sending more troops into Afghanistan. So, I was stuck there for a little while longer. Then I got out. I was able to land a gig as a restaurant manager. Time to get my drinking under control.

# # #

There are twelve-step alcoholics anonymous groups just for veterans. My wife urged me to go. It was not hard to get to Step 1 and say that I am an alcoholic. I don't think it's hard for any of us to get to that point. Or when we say that we are helpless to stop drinking. That, too, is easy. But that third step, committing ourselves to a higher power so that we can stop drinking, that's where it all breaks down. None of us want to stop drinking. All of us are going because someone else wants us to go. A wife, a loved one, maybe a son or daughter. Someone who cannot understand the nightmares. I think that's probably what helps some of us the most. Knowing that we are not alone in our nightmares. We never talk about them. It gives no comfort. We each have our own separate demons. Maybe someone is reliving the slaughter of a friend. And another is reliving the slaughter of a child. And yet another knows the feeling of having a rifle touching the side of his skull and the relief of seeing the body holding the gun riddled with bullets before he can pull the trigger. And you never know what will set off the nightmares. The men I feel most sorry for are the ones whose nightmares come in broad daylight. They are non-functional alcoholics. The ones that AA cannot reach.

I have a mentor who has gotten his nightmares under control. That's what he tells me I need help with. He has even told me his nightmares, and they are unspeakable, except to say that he was infantry. My wife tries to help me. I go fetal at night when I'm not drinking, and she rocks me. Her arms around me sometimes bring me back to the present. Too often, they do not, and I go out and drink again. Sometimes I can go without drinking for a few weeks, sometimes for a few months. They call me a binge drinker now, and I consider that progress. My story is common, except that I have a mentor. There is someone in my life who has actually licked his nightmares. Someday, I hope I will lick my own. But Step Four seems a long way away.

A Flood of Memories

My mother died last week, and I have a myriad of memories of her that I want to share. My earliest ones are the whuppings. Like when she'd whup me for accidentally setting my sister's hair on fire. Not to mention the time I put a snake in the toilet. Or the time she caught me with a telescope looking at the Browns making the bedsprings break next door. I was inquisitive. Mom whupped me a lot.

Now, you have to understand what a whupping is. We're not talking a simple smack on the rear. Oh no. We're talking take your pants off, lie down, take-it-like-a-man whuppings – she used the paddle from the elastic ball paddle toy, after taking the ball off. They were the kind that kept you from sitting down for days, but you had to sit anyway because you couldn't explain it to your teacher. Teacher knew that you did little things, like sticking bubble gum on girls' seats and putting toy cars down the toilet – I loved stopping up toilets - and she wouldn't sympathize. I'm sure you think that fifty years later, I should have gotten over it. I did love her anyway and was in a forgiving mood in my older years, so I could forget some things. I remember the time she wouldn't let me go to the amusement park with my friends AND whupped me, just because of a snake I put in my sister's underwear drawer. We lived next to a creek, so there was an ample supply of snakes.

As time went on, in my teenage years, she became a very interfering mother. I quickly learned not to bring girls home. If I did, she would dig out old photo albums of me in diapers playing with my own poop that I'd scooped out of the back of my butt... and I was really eating it in that most priceless photo. I tried destroying that photo many times. She seemed to have an infinite number of copies because as soon as I'd taken it out of the album and burned it – I love matches - another would pop up. The next thing I knew, the latest girl would be introduced to it, with comments like "wasn't he cute" or worse still, "he was five before he got out of diapers." As if some girl needed to know that I was slow in some forms of development.

So yes, I loved my mother, but she continued to meddle in my love life long after she should have stopped. She would purposely forget girls' names and name the old one or the even older one and sometimes try three or four names of ex-girlfriends before getting it right. Then she would follow it up with, "Oh, are you the one who Martin took to the Bahamas?" and then the girl would expect me to take HER, even if I didn't really like her that way at all.

Yes, I should have learned early that you don't bring your women home to meet your mother, but she would also pop by unannounced, catch me with some woman, hopefully not at the wrong time, but definitely some mornings when a woman would only be at your house because you got some the night before. Then Mom would insist we come for dinner, and of course, said woman would say, "Oh, your mother is so nice." And that would be that; I'd be stuck because you can't fight two women at once. So, there we'd be after Mom had pulled out the photo albums and was making some food that made me drool because my mother's cooking ALMOST made up for some of the whuppings. Mom would invite my lady friend into the kitchen, showing her herbs and, unfortunately, asking nosy questions about her and about me and about how far things had gotten. Mom wanted to know whether she thought things were getting serious and how many children we might have, and then she'd throw in how much she would love a grandchild. Next thing I'd know, she'd be bringing the entire grandmother-wannabe thing up at the dinner table.

And oh, by the way, in case you're wondering where my dad was, he died when I was young. Sometimes, I think it was the smartest thing he ever did because I remember my mother nagging him. I was fifteen when he died and old enough to know nagging when I heard it. "When are you going to take out the trash, fix the garage door, paint the shutters, fix the roof, hang the photos, clean out the basement," or just plain "take a bath," I admit, my dad wasn't keen on bathing twice a day as my mom wanted him to, and it was a bone of contention between them. I think he chose not to take a bath just to spite her, as though that was the only thing he could think of to do that would really get her going. Apparently, it did because there were plenty of times when he slept on the couch, and she probably threw him out of the bed because she was sure he smelled dirty, even when I couldn't tell.

And sometimes Dad just slept on the couch intentionally. Usually, because his favorite team was playing until 11:00 pm on a Sunday or a Monday, Mom would never stand for staying up that late when she had to go teach little brats in middle school and get up at 5:00 am just to be sure to be on top of everything. My dad had a desk job and didn't have to get up until 7:00 am to be at work by 9:00 am, and Mom hated that something awful, so sometimes I think she nagged him just because she envied him. Now I'm not suggesting Dad slept downstairs all the time because I can attest to the fact that there was often some bed-creaking over the kitchen when I would sneak down to see what was in the fridge. Even if there were no moans and groans, I would catch dad smiling on the way out the door; if I got up early enough, mom would hum as she went out the door, and there would be no nagging for a few days. If I was really lucky, I might even get out of a whupping or two while her good mood lasted.

Still, life really changed when my dad died because he had been the one who taught me how to fix things and do manly stuff. It was my dad who taught me how to trap insects and how to fish. Once, he even took me camping with two of my buddies and told ghost stories that made the hair on the backs of our necks stand up. We knew that we had hiked about four miles from the car, and we were in the middle of the woods with no cell phones - because there were no cell phones back then, and there were twitches and noises and crunches and no light and no one except three boys and my dad. We were all nine years old and super susceptible to stories about things that go bump in the night.

At any rate, Dad died of a heart attack when I was fifteen, and my mom acted as though she didn't miss him, but I knew it was a front because sometimes I would catch her crying at night. I let her have her privacy because every once in a while, I would cry and damned if I was ever going to let anyone know.

It turns out that some fifteen years after my dad died, I finally got on mom's right side by marrying and producing grandchildren in that order. I know if I had done it out of order, I would have never heard the end of it, so I made sure to wrap my whopper on the regular. Even if a girl suggested that I go bareback, I would think of my mother and all of the cussing and screaming and carrying on she would do if she found out I had sired a child out of wedlock, so it was just something I made sure I never did.

More than a few young ladies decided that I was quite a catch because I had a degree and worked at a lab, and made good money - I've noticed some women put aside their feelings about who's attractive and who's not when it comes to men with jobs, salaries and cars. So, I was actually in demand by the time I got into my late 20s, and that's when my mom started in with the grandchild stuff.

I married Jeannette at the JP, and I know it infuriated my mother because she had plans to be all decked out. I told her she'd have her chance when my sister got married, and I wanted to spend my money on the honeymoon. We did quite nicely with a trip to Barbados, and the whopper was definitely unwrapped because the first little bundle of joy showed up nine months later, on schedule as far as my mother was concerned.

Actually, it was quite handy that she decided to retire early and become the full-time babysitter for Jolyn and later Chris - and only those two because the tubes got tied, snipped, burned, what-have-you after those two. This was a good thing because Chris was a lot like me.

My mother let me know this constantly. Chris liked to frighten his sister, put his fingers into light sockets, climb into dishwashers, swing on chandeliers after climbing up the chairs in the dining room and just generally act like a four-year-old. Of course, this meant that Jeannette would spank him but not whup him, and my mother changed up on me and would not whup my children. In fact, she would just tell them to wait until we picked them up because she believed she'd done enough disciplining when we were kids, and she would let Jeannette and I handle it in our own way.

I have to give Mom credit. She actually liked Jeanette enough to remember her name, not complain about her cooking - which was just so-so, and most importantly, not meddle in how Jeannette reared our kids. Jeannette reciprocated by asking for advice which made my mother like her more. It was a good thing I had a son because between my mother, my wife and my daughter; I was feeling a bit outnumbered. So, Chris and I would go out a lot and have man time together. I would take him to get his hair cut, show him how to fish and swim and do boy stuff. We even played with snakes since I took him to all of the hands-on museums that my daughter wouldn't be caught dead in. We went to the zoo a lot, to amusement parks and even camping a few times. However, we didn't go nearly as far into the woods as my dad had taken us back when I was nine. Chris wasn't quite up to it until he was much older, and by the time he was older, he was more of a loner than I was. So, I gave him his space and focused on making sure that Jolyn didn't do anything I didn't approve of in the boy department.

When I turned forty, and the kids were eight and nine, my mom started to decline, so I converted the garage into a small studio apartment for her, and she had her own door to come and go as she pleased. She abused this somewhat by sneaking off with men that I thought took advantage of her - even in her seventies, she was still good-looking. I didn't want her to be hurt, although goodness knows she'd been taking care of herself since before I got on the planet. The best thing about having Mom adjacent to us was the fact that she still liked cooking; Jeannette quickly let her take over, and we finally had down-home meals that made you want to go to sleep afterward. This made up for the downside, which was Mom's meddling ways. Before she lived with us, she had been content to let things be, but once she moved in, she found a way to turn me into Dad. Then she convinced Jeannette that I was the handiest man on the planet, and anything Jeannette wanted, I could do. Mom said Jeannette shouldn't hesitate to ask, and in fact, turning to me would save money, even if I really didn't have the time or energy to do some of the things Mom swore I could do. "Take out the trash, fix the back door, paint the shutters, fix the roof, hang the photos, clean out the basement." I'm sure it sounds familiar because it was the same litany she had come up with for Dad, and I suffered through it because Jeanette would back her up every time. You just can't argue with two women who have teamed up against you, so I came up with a rule that requests for things around the house could not be made on Saturday, Sunday or Monday from August to February. This, of course, meant that I could only be asked to do things that took an evening. I am sorry to say that my Fridays and some of my Saturday mornings were spent doing projects that I wasn't even sure were necessary, but I did them so that I could get sex. Yes, I admit that Jeannette would use that trick from time to time, but I'm happy to say that I could make her smile all the way from Friday to Tuesday with my mojo, so that didn't happen very often.

It was only a few years ago, when I turned 50, that mom started going downhill, and it was hard because, well, I was just unprepared for someone who had been such a rock in my life to all of a sudden start to crumble, shrink, stoop and basically wither on the vine the way she did. But she had gotten diabetes and a kidney problem on top of that, and she refused to change the way she ate because, after all, down-home cooking isn't the healthiest, and on top of that, she loved sweets. So, it was not so surprising that if she wasn't willing to give up her ways - and I certainly couldn't make her - then things weren't going to go her way in the health department. So, I watched her decline, but I watched her decline happily at the same time because she was determined to do it her way, and by gosh, it wasn't going to be without sweets or any other wonderful things that she insisted be in her life. Suffice to say, she went faster than she should have, and one day, she just didn't wake up.

I guess I shouldn't say I ever wished her ill, even though she was a stern mother and a challenging housemate. I know, through it all, she loved us. She was good at what she did, and clearly, I didn't turn out half bad, which I give her full credit for, and my sister did fine as well, rounding out her motherly responsibilities. It's easier to man up and say such things than get misty-eyed and maudlin over the simple reality that at some point, it's someone's time to go, and there's no changing that eventuality, so you may as well accept it by the time you've turned 50 as I have. She lived a good life, she knew love, she had the grandchildren she required of us, she had dated long after most, and she ate well. I think perhaps it's easier to remember the whupping and the meddling because then I remember her as she was, with the good and the bad for balance. And that makes it easier.

Me and Mrs. Matthews

"You're going to love Mama. And I know she is going to love you."

I think Michael said this to reassure me, but it didn't work. I could see it coming; a light-skinned girl meets the dark-skinned, overprotective, chip-on-her-shoulder-about-light-skinned-women mother of the guy she's dating. I wanted to believe it would be different, but I had my doubts.

After the hour drive from DC to Baltimore, we arrived at his mother's house. We drove into the driveway, and on cue, Mrs. Matthews came out to meet us. I was stunned; Mrs. Matthews looked so good she could work the blue off a pair of jeans. She wore an up-do of braided locks, had perfect ebony skin, and the kind of lips a white supermodel would pay big bucks for. Her booty made my booty look like the flat side of a ping-pong paddle. She was 59 years old, but she looked 40. I felt woefully inadequate. As Mrs. Matthews gave her son a hug, I stepped out of the car.

"Michael, what's this high yella heifer doin' at my house?" I had nailed it on the head. Nor could I duck back into the car like I wanted to. I wondered what Michael would do to make it worse.

"Mama, this is my girlfriend, Gwendolyn." Here it comes...

"So, she's got one of them high siddity names to go with her high yella skin. Let me guess. She's got a law degree from Harvard." She had me pegged.

"Actually, mama, Gwen's a schoolteacher." *That's right, Michael, stick to the plan. Do NOT tell your mother that I have a law degree from Yale.* That would be like taking a crap on top of a pile of fertilizer. I'm not saying that telling a lie was the brightest idea, but we went for it anyway.

"So, what do you teach?"

"Tenth grade English." I loved English in high school. I could fake this.

"Well, wash up, Michael. Show 'Gwendolyn' where the bathroom is. Dinner's almost ready."

Michael led me into the house. There were intricate carvings of African masks all over the cream-colored walls. Delicious smells of barbecue sauce cascaded through the hallway. We made our way to a first-floor bathroom off the front entrance, and we took turns washing hands. "OK, so it wasn't peanut butter meets chocolate. But she's not so bad once you get to know her."

"Michael, I think she's the one that needs convincing."

Michael and I had been dating for nine months. He'd met *my* parents, and they loved him. He is a blue-black, down-to-the-core black man. Just the way I like them. He has a chiseled jaw, soft eyes, a broad nose, delicious lips - just one scrumptious package of man. He works at an upscale car repair shop as a senior mechanic. That's why I was worried that his mother wouldn't think I'm serious. But I am. He's strong-minded but caring; he brings me flowers for no reason. He listens! To all of the crazy things that happen with my projects. He tells his share of stories at the shop. We banter together; we love each other. We hope to get married. But first, I had to win over his mother.

We met at a gym. One of my girlfriends had talked me into a membership at LA Fitness in Rockville. I wasn't really there to be picked up; I just wanted to join a gym with a pool. But I did notice Michael. He seemed very focused on his workout, so I didn't think he noticed me noticing him. Until one day, he was sitting by the pool, next to my towel.

"Hi, my name is Michael. Want to grab a bite to eat? McDonald's has salads."

Humor. I like that in a guy.

We didn't have schooling in common, but everything else clicked. We shared the same politics; we loved the same music – we knew the same lyrics to the same songs. We both believed in rock-solid finances; we were both saving money for a house. We enjoyed thriller movies and stand-up comedy. We both wanted to go to Africa. We were both considering veganism but couldn't give up bacon and macaroni and cheese. All over lattes and garden salads at McDonald's. It was the craziest first date. And it seriously worked.

Michael met my parents at an annual 4th of July celebration we have at the family beach house in Annapolis - I spent my summers there as a kid. My half-white great-grandfather was probably turning in his grave at the thought of a dark-skinned man inside his beach house, sleeping on his sheets. It was way past time he got over it.

As I mentioned before, my parents loved him. For his sense of humor, the fact that he's a Ravens fan - so's my dad - and of course, because they can see he knows how to treat a woman with respect. Mom told me so when she took me aside and had that mother-daughter talk with me in the kitchen. Luckily, I was old enough not to get the "are you using birth control" question, but she wanted to know more about him. I gave her all the basic dope: age 32, raised in Baltimore, one-parent household, attended Morgan on a football scholarship but had to drop out when he smashed his knee, became a mechanic so he could be near cars, one of his great passions. Then I told her the things we love to do together. We go tandem riding - he bought one after we'd taken a few bike trips together. He has a little boy streak in him, and sometimes at night, we sneak off to playgrounds and play chicken on the jungle gym, seeing who can hold on the longest while we duke it out with our legs. We're pretty evenly matched. We go to all of the parking lot carnivals and get on the rides most likely to make you puke your guts out if you're dumb enough to eat before you go on. He was raised in the church but doesn't go - like me. Plays cards with a passion, doesn't drink, and has never liked drugs. Like me. You wouldn't know we grew up so differently.

To be honest, part of why my mother liked him was because I liked him. Mom's rather easy to please. I found out later that while mom and I were having our talk, Dad was giving Michael the "so what are your intentions with my little girl" talk. Luckily for me, Michael passed. He gave me the high points on our ride home, summarizing with dad's approval. We celebrated by making love on his couch. We celebrate a lot.

Michael's two younger brothers were having dinner with us, along with his mother and his stepfather, Charles, a big bear of a man with close-set ears and a wide smile. Mrs. Matthews set a mean table. There was food everywhere. Plates filled with barbecued ribs, fresh greens, green beans with ham hocks, baked beans, potato salad, and corn on the cob. People passed plates, served each other, and dug in. I had around 10 minutes of quality chewing time before the questions started.

"So, where do you teach?" Mrs. Matthews started. I'd already made up an entire story about teaching at Ballou High School in Anacostia. According to my story, the school was going to be back in session next week, and I was busy decorating my classroom.

"So, do you teach any Shakespeare?" Charles' question caught me off guard, but it was actually quite a lifeline.

"That's my favorite part of the year. We do *The Taming of the Shrew,* and the kids get a big kick out of Petruchio going after Katherine's money and the whole "taming" process. I've tried doing *Midsummer Night's Dream*, but the kids can't get into the fairies."

"I'm surprised you don't do *Othello*," mused Charles.

"Actually, it opens up too many cans of worms. The girls hate the idea of some black guy swooning over a white woman, and the guys are disgusted with how he gets killed in the end. I tried it for one year. Never again."

"So, how long have you been teaching?" Mrs. Matthews asked.

"Seven years now. I really enjoy it." I got into my story. "If you find the right books, the kids can get into it. I actually get them to write a fair amount of poetry, and we have slams in the classroom so they can perform it."

"So, you're teaching at an inner-city school."

"Yes."

"Giving back to the community?"

"Yes."

"Helping the pickaninnies"

"MAMA! That's enough." Michael practically yelled at his mother, and I was embarrassed. I hadn't seen that one coming, but I should have. In fact, I didn't know people even used that word anymore. Guess I was wrong.

I decided to switch gears and get the attention of one of Michael's brothers. "So, Darius, what grade are you going to be in this year?"

"Ninth. We already did Shakespeare. We did *King Lear* last year."

"Really! So, what did you think of it?"

"The two older sisters were seriously ungrateful b-'s, and the King was a dumb a-- for believing their lies." I had to admit; he summed it up pretty well.

"Darius, watch your mouth." Mrs. Matthews put a stop to that conversation.

"Well, she asked."

"Mama," Michael tried this time. "How's the hospital?"

"Actually, it's getting better. They're building a new annex, and maybe it won't be so crowded. Patient care is terrible right now, but I'm trying to bring about some changes."

"What do you do, Mrs. Matthews?" Crap, I did it again. Everyone I knew thought that was such a normal question.

"Michael didn't tell you? I'm the Director of Nursing at the Sinai Hospital in Baltimore. I got my nursing degree from Coppin State 35 years ago - we just had a reunion this past summer. I got it three years before Michael came along."

"Oh wow! My mom's a teaching nurse at George Washington Hospital in DC. You two would probably have a lot in common. She used to come home so tired. My sister and I would rub her feet while she told us about the kids. She worked in the pediatric ward. I was actually a candy stripper before I went to college. I remember how determined mom was that I did not go into nursing, even though I thought she was so wonderful. I think she was happy to see me go into... teaching." Almost blew it.

"Well, I worked my way up in the orthopedic ward. We got a lot of amputees who were trying to get their lives together. Sometimes I felt more like a counselor than a nurse. They needed so much encouragement."

And then Mrs. Matthews began to frown. "Getting to where I am now was a real climb. Affirmative Action came along, and I thought doors would open. But the light-skinned women – like you, Gwen – with less experience kept stepping over me. And then, when I hit 50, I thought they wouldn't promote me because I was too old. If it hadn't been for some amputee kid's father who remembered me nursing his son and happened to be on the Board of Directors, I would have never made it this far. It's downright pathetic when you have to rely on white people because your own people won't pull you up." The waves of anger mixed with sadness emanated from her face. There was nothing I could say.

"So, did you like dinner?" Mrs. Matthews changed subjects.

"It was great. The ribs were to die for, and I haven't had homemade potato salad in a while."

"I'm glad you liked it."

"Can I help you with the dishes?" I think she was shocked I asked. I wanted her to know I didn't mind getting my hands dirty.

"Well, c'mon then. Marcus, clear the table before you go back to your room." Michael had told me that Marcus was a serious gamer.

The kitchen dazzled me; it was obvious that it had been remodeled. The walls were done with an herb motif wallpaper and tile backsplash behind the double sink and the gas stove. There was an island in the center, two ovens, and a huge pantry. The counters were specked marble that matched the stone floors. It was a cook's dream come true.

Mrs. Matthews watched me admire her kitchen. "Charles built it for me after we got married and bought this house. He's a contractor."

"It's beautiful." I gushed. "I'd love to have a kitchen like this someday."

"You're not really a teacher, are you?"

"No, ma'am. I'm a lawyer."

"So why did you lie?"

"Because I thought you'd like me better as a school teacher."

"I don't like liars. Certainly not light-skinned liars with hi sidity names like 'Gwendolyn'".

"I'm sorry, Mrs. Matthews, but I figured you wouldn't like me anyway. I'm surprised you're letting me help with the dishes."

"I have a dishwasher, Gwen; I don't need 'help with the dishes'."

"So, you just wanted to talk to me?"

"Looks like God gave you brains after all."

"I'm sorry you don't like me."

"I'm sorry I don't like you, too. But it looks like I'll have to get used to you. Black wasn't beautiful when I was born, so girls like you gave girls like me a hard time. It stays with you."

"I'm sorry."

"You're sorry about a lot, aren't you? You must be a lousy litigator."

"Actually, I do patent law. I don't argue cases."

"Probably for the best." Mrs. Matthews rinsed the dishes with speed, and I felt pretty useless.

"Why don't I just go back..."

"No, I'm not finished with you. You're a lawyer; Michael's a mechanic. How do you expect to make that work? Or is this just a passing thing for you?"

"No, ma'am, we're quite serious. We hope to get married. I think it depends on you. He loves you very much, and he wants to be with someone you approve of.

"Well then, explain. How do you expect my son to deal with the fact that you make more than he does? What are you going to do when the children come? Who is going to take care of the home, the cooking, the cleaning? How are you going to make sure that my son is the man of the house?"

"Mrs. Matthews, we talk about this, we have talked about this, we will talk about it any time it comes up. Michael likes to cook; I like to clean. Michael fixes things. I'll leave that to him. When children come, I will balance them with my practice. I'm not in court, so I can pick them up if they are sick and work from home if I need to. But most importantly, we treat each other with respect. Decisions will be made jointly. Money will get pooled into a joint account. We're both savers, and we both feel good about our finances. As for him being the man of the house, he will be my man. I'll be his woman. We will be partners.

"At least you've talked about it. At least you've thought about it. It might work. You're not the woman I wanted for my son. I wanted a responsible woman, and I see that you're responsible, but I didn't want a woman who could overshadow him. I'm going to ask that you not rush into this. Wait a few years. Not too long – I want grandbabies. But long enough to know that you've worked through the things that matter."

"Well, 'wait' is not a 'no,' so I think I can live with that. Do you think you'll ever like me?"

"If you give me five grandchildren, I'll like you."

"Five is a lot of grandchildren."

"You've got your work cut out for you."

"I have a lot of respect for you, Mrs. Matthews." I really did.

"He could have done a lot worse. Get going now."

I got gone. Charles and Michael were still at the table, talking politics. I went over and kissed him on the forehead.

"Michael tells me you're a lawyer. Kinda thought so," said Charles.

"My sister teaches. She talks about it constantly, and I really love English."

"Makes sense. My wife's been through a lot, and Michael should have given her some warning about you."

"I've been talking about Gwen for months, Chuck."

"Then I guess you should have sent a picture."

"You're probably right."

"Not that Myra would have liked you any better, Gwen. But at least you'd have gotten a better reception at the front door."

"It's okay. It's happened before."

"Being as light as you are probably brings its share of issues."

"Yes, it does."

"Well, anyone who likes Shakespeare is okay with me." Score one for me.

"Thank you, sir."

"You can call me Chuck."

"OK." Maybe next year.

"Chuck, we have to go." Michael stood up. "I just wanted to bring Gwen by to meet you, but she has a big project she's working on, and she needs to tuck in early."

"I see. Go say goodbye to your mother."

Michael wasn't gone long. As he came out of the kitchen, his mother came out with him. Michael was smiling. I was relieved.

"So, you're leaving?" Asking the obvious.

"Yes, Mrs. Matthews. It was nice meeting you and your family."

"I'm sure I'll see you again."

Michael and I headed out the door, and the ordeal was over.

"See, that wasn't so bad."

"You didn't get called a high yella heifer with a high siddity name."

"True dat. But you handled it."

"Of course, I did. I'm a lawyer."

"So, let's celebrate."

"Sounds like a good idea."

Visitation

"Don't forget my nose candy!" Nana cracked—just one of many drug dealer jokes she'd come up with since Leon was arrested. "I don't know why you're getting all gussied up to see him anyway! Who are you planning to make an impression on—the prison guards?"

Joan Turner looked at herself in the mirror. Even with a touch of make-up, she could see the years starting to show on her face. There were a few age spots on her caramel-colored skin. There were a few wrinkles on her brow. And her lips had lines. She added some lipstick to smooth them out and straightened her navy suit. Maybe she was overdoing it. Who was she trying to impress anyway? Nobody really. She just needed that boost of confidence that looking good brings when you're about to face something difficult like going to visit your son in jail.

She had written letters and sent sketches and drawings from her latest children's books. She sent them every few days. He hadn't written back, and after a while, she hadn't expected him to. Until one day, he did. And asked her to come visit. It was an opening to a door that had been closed ever since he started high school. When sports had taken over his life, and conversations with your mother were just... unnecessary. She continued to feed him, wash his clothes, and even go to his games. But she grew to accept that perhaps teenage boys grew away from their parents. So, the letter had been a surprise and one that she would not ignore.

Still, there was no comeback to her mother's words. Joan hated that. She knew the right reply would come to her a half-hour later when she was already on her way down the road. A two-hour drive from Philadelphia to SCI Frackville with lots of time to think about things. Like, "What had gone wrong?" and even, "Was it something I did?" even if her brain said it wasn't her fault.

Joan could remember the police cars in front of the house in a neighborhood where flashing lights didn't belong. A neighborhood where 80-year-old Mrs. Goldstein walked her Shih-Tzu every night without fear. She remembered the loud, insistent knock on the door: "Open Up, Police." She had felt more embarrassed than afraid. Mrs. Goldstein would probably find a new route for walking the dog. At least the police had waited for Damon to get to the door while she peeked down the stairs in her robe. They were looking for Leon—home from college for the weekend. Joan had never understood why Leon kept coming home on weekends. And she couldn't imagine why the police were looking for him. But Leon seemed to know because he went so patiently. And they found half a kilo of cocaine inside an Air Jordan shoe box.

Damon paid the bail to get his son out of jail, and Joan's brother knew a criminal lawyer who would stall Leon's sentencing until he got through the end of the semester. But Leon had pleaded guilty to possession with intent to distribute. They were hoping that he would be sentenced to less than five years —but he could never go back to Chestnut Hill. What a waste of money. That was how Damon had seen it. There seemed to be no emotion from Damon. Not even anger. Or maybe the emotion was inside where Joan couldn't see it. Was he grieving as she was? Or was it rage? What was the opposite of pride, anyway? Disappointment? All she knew was that it was a topic off-limits, one of so many in their marriage. Even if it was a good marriage, that didn't mean that they could talk about anything she might get emotional about. Damon hated emotion.

And if Damon wouldn't talk about it, he certainly wouldn't go with her. Did fathers visit their sons in jail? What would he and Leon talk about? Or had they ever really had much to say to each other, to begin with? Joan didn't know. Joan wasn't sure that Leon had shut Damon out the way he had closed himself off to her. His grades were okay; he played basketball every winter and worked out the rest of the year. They had gotten him a used car senior year, and he hadn't complained.

So, what went wrong? Or were there too many other things going on for her to have seen it coming? Nana's cancer, Dana's grad school, and Danielle's law school tuition had already added a financial pinch. She was taking on more illustration projects to fill the gaps. There was so much turmoil in the Turner household. Maybe that was it. Or maybe that was just the excuse. Joan got in the car.

Joan loved their neighborhood. They lived on a block with spacious 5-bedroom homes on wooded lots, far enough away from main roads for kids to play basketball in the driveways without worrying about fast cars. Women jogged every hour of the day. Now the Christmas trees were out at the curb, waiting for post-holiday pick-up. She turned right on Lockhill and counted three snowmen, two snowball fights, and an igloo as she covered the four blocks to the main road. Finally, the neighborhood fell away, and the strip malls began. A grocery store, a Costco. And then onto the highway. The long drive began at that point, and Joan had too much time to think.

"Two out of three ain't bad, Nana." That was the comeback she couldn't come up with before she went out the door. Two out of three were overachievers, and Leon was just a normal boy, outshone by miles. Leon probably hadn't stood a chance. She thought they had given him his share of attention. They had been going to his basketball games since middle school. They stitched him up when he fell, wrapped him up when he broke a bone, nursed him through mono, and got him through adolescence and into college. He didn't bring home girls, and no angry fathers called to say that a daughter was pregnant, so Joan figured Damon had at least hammered that message home. It was strange that it seemed like an empty nest after the twins had gone off to college, even though Leon was still home. The girls were more talkative, or perhaps they simply talked to her more. Leon wasn't into confiding. So, the house was quiet. Leon didn't even play music in his room. He simply walked around with an iPhone and earphones when he was home, which wasn't much. Another reason why they didn't talk. Leon always seemed to have a separate life. Joan took an exit onto the Interstate. She knew that money was tight, and Leon had probably felt it. By the time he was a senior in high school, they'd had four straight years with two kids in college. Hence the used car. Damon made good money, but that just meant no scholarships. And her attention to Leon had dipped even more sharply when Nana had moved in. Joan had no idea what was going on in Leon's head. She wasn't even sure that she knew him anymore. Perhaps she'd find out who he was when she saw him.

Driving through the prison gates was a culture shock. She could see the barbed wire and the turrets where men with guns overlooked the yard. As she walked into the lobby, she could feel the oppressiveness of the gray walls. The lobby was crowded with people who looked tired. There were four young women with what seemed like swarms of children, including two infants —wives or girlfriends, she couldn't know. The three women who looked like mothers seemed worn out from life. And there were no men at all. No fathers, no brothers, no friends. She wasn't the only one dressed nicely, but the only one in a suit. She was a fish out of water.

As she signed in, Joan wondered what she had been thinking. Her name was called, and she steeled herself to go through the door, to have her purse checked, her body scanned. But it was nothing like going through airport security. She realized that when she heard the clang of the steel door closing behind her. They had frisked her, their hands creeping over her legs and chest, searching for something she'd never dreamed of carrying. And through it all, there was the sense of aloneness as she was processed, all by herself, with no safety in numbers as there was at the airport—where everyone was so obviously going through the same thing. At last, it was over, then through another security door and down a corridor to a room with glass walls where Leon waited.

Her son was wearing the uniform of a prisoner. His acne had broken out, and he looked young. But still defiant. As if she was there to judge him, and he dared her to try to understand him. And because of that, she was hesitant. The armor of her navy suit was pierced, and she felt tears on the inside.

She sat down, with her hands clutching her purse, not knowing where to begin. "How are you?" So cliché.

"I'm alright, Mom. There were a few fights, just to gain respect and keep the punks at arm's length. Nothing really unexpected. The food is lousy, and it's actually pretty boring in here. How's Nana?"

Nana was a topic she could handle. She began to talk about taking Nana to chemo, but not the vomiting attacks that followed. She told him about Nana's growing collection of chic wigs and the newest style with magenta streaks on the side. There seemed no point in mentioning that Nana was starting to stoop over or how much her veins were showing. After a while, she realized that she was rambling.

"Nana's fine, Leon."

"And what does Dad have to say?"

"Nothing new. Muttering about paying the bills, angry that the Eagles didn't make the playoffs."

"About me, Mom."

"Oh. Nothing really. He sends his love." She lied.

"Right. And pigs fly. It's okay, Mom. He is who he is. How about you? How are you doing?"

Once again, she rambled on, telling him about her latest illustration project. It was going to be a book about a little boy who builds snowmen so that he can have imaginary playmates. She was so happy to be working with a black author. It was rare, and she couldn't be picky. She stopped herself after a while.

"I'm fine, Leon." Another lie.

"So, I'm the only one who's not fine. I'm here, and I hate it, and it doesn't matter because I'm stuck here anyway, so I do what I'm told, read when allowed, sleep when allowed, shit and piss when allowed...and just keep my head down. No point in calling attention to myself." Leon leaned forward.

"You know, Mom, what I really miss in here...it's weird. I don't miss TV or my music or gaming or anything like that. I miss being on a team. Where people have your back. Nobody does anything for you in here unless there's something in it for them. It's sick, actually. This is a sick place."

"Leon, how did you end up here? What were you thinking—I mean, well, what did we do wrong?"

"You didn't do anything wrong, Mom; I was broke, I wanted spending money, the kids wanted drugs, I supplied them. It was really that simple."

"How did you fall in with those people?"

"I didn't fall in with anyone special, Mom; they were just there, I was there, it fit together. Don't you remember college, Mom? Weren't there drugs?"

Joan paused. She didn't remember anything like that in college. The only craziness she remembered was the stories of who was sleeping with whom; she had stuck to the on-campus parties, trying to have fun without getting caught up in the sexual escapades of her friends. And then she had fallen in love with Damon and stopped paying attention to anything else.

"I guess you never noticed. Dad always wanted it that way, Mom. He said that was what a man was supposed to do for his woman. That's why we moved so many times. So that you would always be in a safe neighborhood, and he taught us all to shelter you. If I got into fights, or got drunk or got in trouble, I was supposed to keep you out of it. Whatever kind of girl I was spending time with or sleeping with, I wasn't supposed to bring her home. He wanted you to have it like that, to think the world was a good place and that we were good kids. And I blew it. Big time. Even now, I'm telling you things you're not supposed to know."

Joan felt socked in the stomach. All these years, she had thought they were moving because Damon wanted a bigger house. All these years, she'd been happy to think that her kids had perfect lives. It was all an illusion. And now she was facing a Leon she hadn't known existed. A part of her wanted to pull away, but instead, she leaned closer to reach out to him. But the glass plate was in the way. Leon went on.

"Drugs are everywhere, Mom, especially on campus. Sure there are classes, but there's pressure, and you want release, so you take something for release, and you want something to help you through exams, so you take something for that, and then you just want to forget, so you take something to forget. If you have money, it can be that way. After I figured it out, figured out who wanted it, where to get it, how to sell it, well, I had money too. I think you forgot what college is like when everyone has money except you."

Joan thought back again. Nobody had money in her circle. Everyone was trying to get ahead; no one had time for drugs or money for drugs. No, she thought again. There were some kids with money. They would head to the slopes for winter break, head to Florida for spring break, and head off campus for entertainment. They had cars. Nobody in her circle had a car. Maybe those kids took drugs. She actually didn't know. She shook her head.

"Mom, just leave it alone. It happened, I got caught, I'm in here. And you're seeing me as I am. It doesn't make you a bad mother. You were a great mother. Dad was a great father. So, stop looking for some way to take the blame when it isn't yours."

Joan felt the tears rise, finally admitting to herself that she'd needed to be absolved. That she needed it not to be her fault. But if it wasn't her fault, and it wasn't Damon's fault, then it was Leon's fault. "You're not a bad kid, Leon."

"Yes, Mom, I am. I'm a drug dealer. I would show up to parties with some cocaine or ludes, then sit back and wait for rich kids to get addicted to it. Then they'd have to keep coming back no matter how much it cost. That's what I was doing. And I own it. Nobody's in here by mistake, Mom. Not me, not the guy next to me, none of us. Trust me, I can tell. The guys in here are nothing like the people you know. Nothing like the calm, pretty world you lived in before your son ended up in prison. This is my life now, Mom. And I'll be a felon for the rest of my life. When I get out of here, doors will get slammed in my face. No one hires felons; good colleges and college basketball teams don't want felons; decent parents don't let their daughters date felons. It's like having it tattooed on my forehead."

"It's going to be a mess, isn't it?"

"It's already a mess, Mom. But if I can survive here, I can survive out there. Trust me. I'll find a way to finish school. I'll start a business. I'm actually a pretty good businessman already. I've mastered supply and demand. So, I'll make my way. Is that what you've been worried about? My future?"

"Yes, I guess so. I wanted great things for you."

"Time's up, ma'am." The interruption shattered her. She and Leon had never talked this much, ever. She was starting to face his manhood, learning who he really was, not understanding but hoping to find a way to accept him as he was, even if she couldn't accept how he saw himself.

"Leon, I'll come again. I won't wait until you ask me."

Joan could see Leon wipe his eye. "I love you, Mom. Thanks for coming. It meant a lot to see you. To talk to you. To have a connection."

As Joan walked out the door, she thought about everything Leon had said. Even though her world view had crumbled, she still wasn't a bad Mom...It was as if he'd forgiven her for being who she was. A very naïve woman in a very complicated world. She got into her car as the tears flowed freely.

Transformations

February 1st -

Dear Celia,

I miss you so much. Why did you have to move away? I thought we would be together forever. Now you're in New York, and I'm stuck here in po-dunk Iowa. And we were doing so well. Walking the mall, eating our smoothies, drinking our diet sodas. I lost 30 pounds, and then, in the time you've been gone, I put it all back and then some. I've now hit 350 pounds in 6 months. I truly am Bess the Cow. I've just got to do something, but I don't know what. I've tried Weight Watchers, I've tried Atkins. But they just don't fit into my lifestyle. My oh-so-thin husband complains if I change what we eat, and I watch him dive into his food with such gusto that I end up having more than I should. I swear, I will never master portion control. But I have to do something. I'm 39 years old, and I am sick and tired of being fat.

Missing you,

Bess

February 7th,

Dearest Bess,

A letter! I haven't gotten a letter in so long. Everyone is always doing phone calls and text messages. But a letter. You made my day. Work is super crazy. Did I really say I wanted to do corporate law? I must have been crazy. The caseload is wicked; the hours are horrendous, and the expectations on me are insane. And yet, I love it. I think the only thing about Iowa that I miss is you. And my parents, of course. I miss our walks; I miss our talks. I miss our smoothies. I miss your encouragement – it made law school bearable, knowing that you believed in me on those days when I just wanted to give up. We're in the 21st century, and white men still can't accept black women in law school.

But enough about me. YOU! You are going to turn this around. I just know it. If there's anything you can think of that would help, let me know.

I love you.

Celia.

February 14th -

Dear Celia,

I've found this old book in the used bookstore called "Fit for Life", and it talks about veganism. According to the book, if you give up animal products and don't eat fatty foods like potato chips, you can lose weight without portion control. Oh gawd, I want this. But Jeff will have a massive fit. He'll never give up his meat and cheese. Can you imagine him without steak and fried chicken? Never. I'll have to cook separate meals. I know it's going to drive me crazy. But I really want this. Celia, do you think you could help me. Maybe send little encouraging postcards? I don't know if I can do this alone. Let me know.

Bess

February 28th -

Dear Celia,

I've decided to go cold turkey. Nuts and berries. Actually, there are fat bears... I'm not sure about this, but I've tried everything else. I stuck a wad of stamped postcards in here. If you could just send one every other week, I know it would make a difference.

Bess

March 7th –

Hey Bess,

I can't write much, but I promise you'll always hear from me. I've heard great things about veganism. Don't think I could do it, but it's certainly worth a try. Keep me posted. I'm rooting for you all the way.

Love C.

March 14th -

Dear Celia,

You're not going to believe this. It's been two weeks, and I've lost 15 pounds. That tightness in my clothes is gone. It's so wonderful. And that postcard made my week because Jeff is acting really strange. I'm still cooking everything he loves, but he used to come into the kitchen, wrap his arms around me, and whisper, "I love my moo-moo." He doesn't do it anymore, and I really miss that.

Bess

March 21st -

Hey Bess,

Wow! 15 pounds. That's terrific. Make sure you take vitamins. I was reading about veganism, and that seems to be important. And Jeff - he'll come around. Remember that he loves you.

Love C.

March 28th -

Dear Celia,

I lost another 5 pounds, but nuts and berries are getting boring. I'm going to have to figure something else out. Spaghetti with marinara sauce (with some meatballs for Jeff). Stir-fried veggies – with some shrimp for Jeff. I looked online for a support group, but nothing fits.

Weight Watchers and Atkins preach portion control. And PETA folks are so fanatic. I'm not trying to save the planet. I just want to lose weight. I guess I'm going it alone. At least I have you. Loving your postcards.

Bess

April 4th -

Hey Bess,

Five more pounds! Yippee! There seem to be more and more black Vegans these days. See if there's a Facebook group with recipes. Or consider Pinterest. Maybe Google "Vegan recipes that you can add meat to" so that you can cook for you and Jeff at the same time. But whatever you do, stay the course! Twenty pounds! You're awesome.

love you back. C.

April 11th -

Dear Celia,

I lost another 5 pounds, and I'm finding cookbooks with interesting recipes. Seems it's all about beans. Baked beans, beans and rice, beans in chili... and Beano. Because Jeff is seriously complaining about the gas; sometimes he sleeps on the couch. But I'm under 325 pounds. I wish he would support me. Please keep those postcards coming.

Bess

April 18th -

Hey Bess,

Can't write much this week but know that I'm thinking about you. You're courageous; you're moving forward; you're doing this! Go you!

C.

April 25th -

Dear Celia,

I've lost 30 pounds, and my clothes are super loose. People are starting to notice, and it feels good. I could never tell Jeff; I know he would be angry. But Celia, I'm starting to think that I could lose some serious weight. Maybe 50 pounds. Maybe more. I can't remember being under 300 pounds. It's been so long. Jeff has never known me under 300 pounds. I guess this is too much change for him. Do you remember me under 300 pounds?

Bess

May 2nd -

Dear Bess,

It's definitely been a while since you were under 300 lbs. Back in college, I think. But know this - whatever your weight, you are beautiful; if you want to get under 300 lbs., go for it. I know you can do it.

C.

May 9th -

Dear Celia,

I lost another 5 pounds and got a haircut. Jeff is furious. I never realized how much long hair meant to him. But the braids got heavy; and a perm is such a pain. I love me au naturelle. Did you know I've got some curl? I'm going to get professional photos. Glamour Shots. Dammit, I feel good about myself. He's just going to have to cope.

Bess

May 16th -

Hey Bess,

I can't wait to see the photos with the new do! I'm so excited for you! Keep on keepin' on.

C.

May 23rd -

Dear Celia,

Check out these photos! I got my Glamour Shots, and they gave me a makeover. I've never really tried make-up before. Real foundation and everything. I love the look. I think I'm going to sign up for a class. I want to learn how to do this for myself, and they have a program for 4 weeks on Monday nights. That can be Kentucky Fried Chicken night for Jeff. And I lost another 5 pounds.

Bess

May 30th -

Hey Bess,

These photos look awesome! You're amazing! And I can see the weight loss. You're really doing this! I knew you could. Just keep believing in yourself.

C.

June 6th –

Dear Celia,

I lost 5 more pounds. I'm under 310, and for the first time in years, I can see my toes. So, I went and got a pedicure. Sat in the chair and felt those massage balls go up and down my back. Put my feet in the water just like a Jacuzzi, felt strong hands up and down my calves, and could feel the slough come off my heels. My feet are so soft. I decided to get French tips. With a little V., I feel so sexy. I've really been neglecting myself. It's time to change that.

Bess

June 13th -

Hey Bess,

Yes, pedicures are a gift from the goddess, and you deserve to get them. Let them be a regular reward. You deserve it!

C.

June 20th –

Dear Celia,

I lost 5 more pounds, and I've decided to re-invent myself. I'm giving myself a new name. Bessie is a name for a cow. I'm going to be BeBe. Let me know what you think. I've been practicing it on a piece of paper, I've changed my name on Facebook, and I'm going to get personalized stationery and send it to everyone I can think of. Goodbye, Bess. Hello, BeBe! With a picture of my Glamour Shot. I'll be the talk of the family reunion.

BeBe

June 27th -

Hey

BeBe,

A totally fabulous new name for the new you! I love it!

C.

July 4th -

Dear Celia,

I DID IT! I've lost 50 pounds. It's hard to believe. But it's for real. I'm down to 300 pounds. I'm going to take pictures of the scale and post them on the wall. I need to really celebrate this, but I'm not sure how. In the past, I've always celebrated with food. I don't even want to. I don't want to mess with my success. So, maybe a facial and a full body massage. Gotta take care of this new body. But Celia, I've got to tell you. Jeff is acting worse and worse. It's like he doesn't want me to lose the weight. I thought he'd be happy for me. Not sure what to do. Last year, I would have eaten a bucket of chicken or a gallon of ice cream. Today – a mixing bowl full of lettuce with balsamic vinaigrette.

BeBe

July 11th -

Hey BeBe,

Jeff has never seen you less than 300 lbs., but you can't let him get to you. Just keep going.

C.

July 18th -

Dear Celia,

I've lost 5 more pounds. So, it's time to buy new clothes. Not sure why I put it off. Maybe because I don't trust what's happening, and I don't know if I can keep the weight off. But this has got to be part of my reinvention. And I'm going to buy some dresses. I'm starting to have a waist, and I want to show it off. Not sure to whom, but I do. No more tents for clothing. And no more fat cow catalogs. I fit into a size 26. Hello Dress Barn Woman and Lane Bryant. Goodbye Catherines and size 5X. In fact, I think I'm going to buy a suit. Just one. I've always wanted to go to church in one of those beautiful white suits. Maybe even a hat. Re-invention.BeBe.

July 25th

Hey BeBe,

A hat! You have got to send pictures. You're fabulous!

C.

August 1st -

Dear Celia,

There's a job opening for a marketing manager. I'm going to go for it. I've been at this job for so long; I've gotten every kind of project and everyone says I've handled them well. I'm good at what I do, and I deserve this. And I now look the part. I wear a dress to work every day with some make-up, I don't frown so much, people have noticed the changes in me, and I've shown that if I put my mind to something, I can do it. Do you realize what an accomplishment it is to lose 60 pounds? Yup, I lost 5 more. I want this job so badly I can taste it.

BeBe

August 8th -

Hey BeBe,

You've put in the time; you know what to do. It's already yours.

C.

August 15th -

Dear Celia,

I got the job! I'm going to be the marketing manager. And they've doubled my salary. I'm even making more than Jeff. I wish he'd be happy for me. All he can think about is that I might have to do overtime and whether I'd still be home in time to make dinner. It can't always be about him, can it? Still, I am doing this for myself. He never told me that he wanted me to lose weight. I was always his "Little Moo-Moo." He won't even call me BeBe. And when we go out, he's constantly looking around and saying stupid little things like, "He may be looking at you, but all he wants is sex." I don't even see when men look at me. And that's not why I'm doing this. Dammit, I want to be healthy. Do you know what it's like when you go to step on the scale at the doctor's office, and they pull out a special scale? Or when you get the "obesity talk" with scare stories about diabetes, high cholesterol, and heart attacks? He just doesn't understand. And it hurts, Celia. It really hurts.

BeBe

P.S. Five more pounds.

August 22nd -

Hey BeBe,

I hear your pain but keep going anyway. Your health is just as important as your husband. Take care of you.

C.

August 29th -

Dear Celia,

My skin is starting to flab on me. I think it's time to go to the gym. Not sure when to fit it in. Maybe after dinner. Or in the morning before work. I'm debating between Planet Fitness,

Golds Gym, and Bally's. Planet Fitness has the best hours, but Bally's has a pool. Can you imagine! Me in a bathing suit! Yup, that's it. Bally's. It will give me added incentive. And I lost 5 more pounds.

BeBe

September 5th -

Hey BeBe,

Rock that swimsuit! Don't forget to take pictures. Make sure it's a flattering color. No drab, basic black. Go wild!

C.

September 12th -

Dear Celia,

I'm going to the gym twice a week, evenings, while Jeff is on his PlayStation, and I lost 5 more pounds. I don't understand why he's so angry all the time. When I showed him my swimsuit - a modest one-piece suit with a high neck and a little skirt - he lost his ever-loving mind. Called me a whore and a slut and all kinds of other names too sick to mention. Said I wanted to be raped again. I almost changed my mind about going. I think that's what he wants, for me to lose my nerve and go back to being Bess the Cow. But I can't. I've come so far. My life is changing in unimaginable ways. I feel good about myself. I didn't realize it before, but it's new to me, this feeling. That I can do anything, be anything. OK, maybe not an astronaut, but you know what I mean. And I want this for myself. I deserve this. I am a beautiful person, inside and out, and I love me. It feels weird to say it, but I love me. And Jeff can just go to hell.

BeBe

September 19th -

Hey BeBe,

I'm glad you're loving you. I love you, too. And I agree; if Jeff can't be supportive, he can go to hell.

C.

September 26th -

Dear Celia,

It's probably TMI, but I'm realizing that Jeff and I haven't been together in about 3 months. I think it was when I hit 325 pounds. It's as though he thinks I've become ugly. I want him to love me the way he used to. But I'm not sure I can make that happen and still be the new BeBe. I think he's going to make me choose. Would it be selfish if I chose myself? I don't know how to win him back without putting the weight back on. And I refuse. I just can't do it. Not and be true to me. I will never again be Bess the Cow. I guess we need counseling.

BeBe

P.S. Lost 5 more pounds.

October 3rd -

Hey BeBe,

I think you're making the right choice. Jeff could die tomorrow. Nothing in life is certain. Be true to yourself.

C.

October 10th -

Dear Celia,

I suggested marital counseling, and Jeff laughed in my face. He wanted to know what good it was going to do. He said he never wanted me to change. He never asked for me to change. I didn't know I needed his permission. I've tried to keep some things the same. I made sure I still came home on time. I made sure to have his dinner ready. But it's just not good enough. He says he hates the new me. The new look, the new name, the new job, the new weight. That I'm not the woman he married. And he said I'm not changing for the better as far as he's concerned. I was surprised when he threw in the new job. Could that be a piece of it? That I make more than he does? It hasn't changed me! Or maybe it has. I spend more on myself. And I don't ask his permission because I don't have to ask him for money. Yup, that's probably a big piece of it. Somehow, I have to get him to counseling.

BeBe

P.S. I lost another 5 pounds.

October 17th -

Hey BeBe,

Jeff was always like that. You just didn't see it, and I didn't say anything. Being married was very important to you. But this new you is very important, too. Don't sacrifice yourself for him.

C.

October 24th -

Dear Celia,

I bought myself some Spanx to hold in the loose skin, and I'm thinking of getting surgery to cut the excess skin off. You wouldn't believe how much it costs. And it's cosmetic surgery. Insurance doesn't cover it. That's so unfair. I would have to take out a loan. I'm going to wait and see how much weight I actually lose. No point in doing it now. I lost another 5 pounds.

BeBe

October 31st -

Hey BeBe,

Start saving while you're shrinking. And when the time comes, every penny will be worth spending. Be patient, knowing that when it's the right time, it will happen.

C.

November 7th

Dear Celia,

I did it! I've lost 100 pounds! I'm 250 pounds. I can't even remember a time when I was under 250 pounds, sometime in my twenties. It was before I met Jeff; he never knew me when I was thinner. I guess he likes fat women. Broke women. Women with no self-esteem. Everything I don't want to be anymore. So, I guess he can't love me anymore. It hurts, Celia. I think I'll eat some watermelon. An entire watermelon.

BeBe

November 7th -

Hey BeBe,

Change is painful, but seriously, you've got this. Watermelon sounds safe. Even an entire watermelon. Don't forget about the pedicures.

C.

November 14th -

Dear Celia,

I think Jeff is having an affair. At the same time, I go to the gym. He's started encouraging me to go. Nothing else makes sense. Why would he do this to me? I've tried to be the best wife I know how to be. Celia, I still love him. Maybe that seems crazy given everything he's said, but he's been my rock for so many years. Would you believe we've almost been married for 15 years? And he's stuck by me through so much. When we found out that I couldn't have children, he didn't leave me, and he could have. When they found that tumor, he was right by my side, that time I got raped in the park, he didn't blame me or back away. So much. And just because I want something for myself, he wants to rip it all away. It doesn't make any sense. I wish I could have some ice cream. Watch me eat another watermelon.

BeBe

November 21st -

Hey BeBe,

You are woman! Don't cry, roar! You've handled so much; you've dealt with so much. You can deal with this too. I promise it will work out.

C.

November 28th -

Dear Celia,

I was right. Jeff is having an affair. We lost power at the gym, so I went home early. I could hear the bed creaking from the front door. You would think that I'd be mad. I was just curious. And when I got to the bedroom, I was shocked. She was the biggest woman I'd ever seen. He was slapping her and saying, "who's my cow?" He was so filled with anger, and she was taking it. And maybe I'm seeing him as he is for the first time. It's so important for him to be dominant that he has to be with a woman with low self-esteem. Celia, that's not me anymore. So, I guess that's what it is. I walked away. I don't think they even knew I was there. I'm staying in a hotel. All 240 pounds of me.

BeBe

December 5th -

Hey BeBe,

Be strong. You've done all of this without his support. Maybe you're outgrowing him. I love you!

C.

December 12th -

Dear Celia,

This guy at work hit on me today. It was so weird. He's one of the hottest men in the department. And lawdamercy, the thought of having sex with him is enough to make me come all over myself. But I'm still married. To a lying, cheating, no-good son of a b----, but married is married. I wonder if I would take him up on it if I was single. I don't think so. I'm not the one-night type. I think I deserve better. Someone I can get to know, spend quality time with... then sex. Look at me. I'm already thinking about being single. Maybe it's time to talk to a lawyer.

BeBe

December 19th -

Hey BeBe,

You made the right choice. No one-night stands. That's not you. Don't change your values. But yeah, definitely time for a lawyer.

C.

December 26th -

Dear Celia,

I'm down to 235 pounds, and it's time for new clothes again. And new Spanx. I'm a size 20, and it feels so good. I'm not fat; I'm curvy!

Sure, the doctor may call me obese, but I know what I was, and that's not me anymore. I am BeBe Lawson. Young, successful, beautiful. Jeff be damned.

BeBe

January 2nd -

Hey BeBe,

That's my girl! Send some new pics. I want to see all the new clothes! And I want to hear about that lawyer!

C.

January 9th -

Dear Celia,

Jeff said the craziest thing to me. He told me that if I would eat a pork chop, he'd stay with me. So, I had a bite. Just to see. And I nearly threw up. In that bite of pork chop was everything that I had been and never wanted to be again. In that bite of porkchop was Bess the

Cow. I may be vegan for life! Never again prime rib, never again macaroni and cheese, never again sour cream on a potato, never again a bowl of Cap'n Crunch, never again a Hershey's bar, never again Nacho Cheese Doritos. Never again, Bess the Cow. It's a fair trade.

BeBe

January 16th -

Hey BeBe,

I am SO proud of you. You answered many important questions. You're not going to quit; you're not going to let Jeff dictate who you are. You're not going to stop changing and growing – yes, you're growing.

C.

January 23rd -

Dear Celia,

I'm 225 pounds, and I think I'm ready to see someone about the surgery now. Maybe it sounds crazy, but I'm okay if I stay at 225. I'm a size 18, squarely in Women's Plus, but if I don't get down to 200, I'll be okay. I want to tell you something crazy. All those postcards you send – I keep them in a scrapbook. I put gold frames around them with little flowers or hearts or stars. And at the top of the page, I put my weight in fancy digits from Michaels. The numbers keep dropping, and when I'm struggling, I just open up the scrapbook, and there you are, encouraging me. I could have never done this without you.

BeBe

January 30th -

Hey BeBe,

It was all you; I'm just along for the ride. But hey, since I know this will be immortalized, here are a few important words. Love yourself. Keep going. You've got this. You're beautiful. As one door closes, so many more will open. Again, you've got this.

C.

February 6th -

Dear Celia,

I guess I'm not done yet. I lost another 5 lbs. I think I'm scared to stop losing because I'm afraid I'll start gaining. I went for my annual physical, and my doctor nearly fainted away. She was so proud of me. She has referred me to a nutritionist who might be able to help me figure out how to keep the weight off forever. No backsliding. Not BeBe.

February 13th -

Hey BeBe,

Sounds like a plan. Keeping it off is as important as taking it off. I'm so proud of you!

C.

February 20th -

Dear Celia,

Jeff filed for divorce. Irreconcilable differences. I know it's been coming, but I still can't say that word. Divorce. And I'm so tempted to eat something unhealthy. To stuff my face, to have everything I've denied myself all year. But I'm not going to do it. Look how far I've come. New name, new look, new job... it never occurred to me that all that change would be too much for Jeff. Or that he would want to hold me back. I didn't realize he was so insecure. He wants to marry Julia, the woman he's been cheating with. He says he wants to wear the pants; he doesn't want me to make more than he does, he doesn't want me to be more attractive than he is, he wants to be better than me, and if he can't feel that way, he doesn't want to be with me. He's letting me keep the house. He just wants the retirement account. I guess that's fair.

BeBe

February 27th -

Hey BeBe,

I know that being married was very important to you, and having Jeff's support through all the craziness in your life has been a godsend. But his attitude toward the new you was unhealthy, unsupportive, and downright un-husbandly. In sickness or IN HEALTH. So, he was supposed to love you healthy. For RICHER or poorer. So, he was supposed to love you when you're making more money. He failed the marriage test. Not you. You are going to be just fine without him. Keep saying it until you believe it.

C.

March 6th –

Dear Celia,

I have the house to myself, and it's too big for me. I'm going to sell it. Buy a condo. Maybe get a dog. Maybe take a cruise. They say that women take a cruise when they get a divorce. Or go to an island. Get my groove back. But I don't want a man. The compliments are nice, but being sexy wasn't really my goal, was it? I've never turned heads before. In fact, I was never with a man before Jeff. No one ever loved me before Jeff. And I'm no longer sure he loved me. He may have been too insecure to love anyone. Well, it's time to get BeBe's head on straight. A cruise. Oh, and I'm down to 210 pounds.

BeBe

March 13th -

Hey BeBe,

Have a great time, you deserve it.

C.

March 20th -

Dear Celia,

I've just gotten back from my cruise. No, I didn't meet a man. But I splurged on every possible excursion. I went snorkeling, played with stingrays, saw some Mayan ruins, and bought jewelry. I did everything but eat. And let me tell you, being vegan on a cruise is hard. But I did it. Vegan for life. It isn't what I planned. I just wanted to lose the weight. But I don't want to go back to 350 pounds, and I don't know any other way to keep it off... except for portion control, and I was never good at that. No, I'm just going to be one of those rabbit food eaters. And would you believe I lost 5 pounds on the cruise?

BeBe

March 27th -

Hey BeBe,

It's all about lifestyle changes. Living proof. I'm so glad you had a good time. Pictures???? Tell me you got one of you with the stingray.

C.

April 3rd -

Dear Celia,

Can you believe it, I'm down to 200 pounds? I got a chocolate lab named Charlie. I take him on long walks twice a day. He sleeps with me and keeps me company. And life doesn't seem so empty. You may not hear from me so often, but I can't thank you enough for letting me tell you what's been happening to me. You've been a rock, and I love you for it. If there's ever anything that you're going through, write to me, and I promise to listen.

Best wishes,

BeBe

Snapped

Tiesha greeted her prospective stepfather with a carving knife. She was only ten and still in love with her father. Ray had been warned but still hadn't expected the knife. Tiesha waved it toward his penis in a circling motion as though she knew exactly how Ray felt about her mother and was willing to put a stop to it. Ray had to admit that sex with Wanetta was something he thoroughly enjoyed, but he couldn't believe it was that obvious. His penis, acting defensively, shriveled up into a stub and clung to his leg for dear life.

"Tell me why I should like you," said Tiesha.

There wasn't any good answer. "Because I love your mother" wouldn't do. In fact, that was irrelevant and possibly irritating. Definitely unwelcome and could even be fatal. Ray's hesitation wasn't helping either.

"I'm a nice guy." Lame but non-threatening. "And I like jigsaw puzzles." Wanetta had mentioned that this was Tiesha's favorite pastime whenever computers and cellphones were off-limits. Ray wished he had brought one. But he noticed the knife start to droop. This was a good sign.

"What would you like me to do besides go away?" This was a gamble, but it was all Ray could think of.

"You could give me a billion dollars." Mercenary little thing. Ray stifled a laugh.

And his savior finally appeared.

"Tiesha, what the... what are you doing?" Wanetta was coming down the stairs, and Ray had that feeling he always got when he looked at her. She had rich brown perfect skin, deep-set eyes, full kissable lips, and curves everywhere that mattered. She wore a cute gym suit. She didn't wear fancy clothes on the weekends, which had made it easier on him. His son's mother was robbing him blind, and it helped that Wanetta wasn't financially demanding. The plan was to go to the park where they were having a street carnival. Funnel cakes, rides, games. Ray wasn't excited about the rides but had been warned that he had to get on at least a few of them to make the grade.

Wanetta was fast, and Tiesha was grabbed from behind by two encircling arms that had her by the wrists, putting the knife out of commission. "Drop it. Now." The knife fell on the floor. Ray assumed Wanetta's grip was pretty tight. Wanetta crossed her arms around her daughter's chest, pulled her close, and whispered something in her ear. Tiesha's face fell to the floor, and Ray couldn't imagine what had been said. Raising boys was not the same. You stared them down. There wasn't anything said. Time outs didn't work anyway. A look of momentary disgust that said, "You disappoint me," when a son craved approval. Ray didn't even have to do it very often. It was too powerful. And he loved his son. He wished he didn't hate his son's mother so much. You never really know a woman until you divorce her

Tiesha had evidently been raised right because she muttered an "I'm sorry" before she ran back up the stairs. Ray wasn't sure whether the park was a bust. Sometimes it had to be that way.

Wanetta gave Ray a brief kiss, then stood back quickly. She had also warned him that she wouldn't be affectionate in front of Tiesha, something he had to accept. She invited him into the living room and got him a beer.

It wasn't the first time Ray had been to the house. He had come over when Tiesha was with her father. But he hadn't noticed much on the way to the bedroom. Wanetta had that effect on him. When she was around, he didn't notice much else. The house was like an art gallery with pieces by Barnes, Goodnight and other famous artists displayed on the walls. A weaving of rich colors hung over the mantle place above the usual mélange of family pictures. An entertainment center with a modest-sized TV took up a wall of the living room, still blending in with the floor. There was a sense of the understated. The floors were rich amber hardwood. The kitchen had white cabinets and steel appliances. The entire effect was one of a respectable income. An "I don't need your money – I'm doing just fine on my own" kind of house. Half comforting, half intimidating. In a way, you knew where you stood with Wanetta. She either liked you as a person, or she didn't. Income wasn't going to impress her. Ray wasn't even sure he made as much as she did. They didn't talk about it. It was strange. He knew all about her job – she was a buyer for a clothing chain. She said she hated to dress up on the weekends because she had to dress-to-impress throughout the week. Ray had seen her during the week when she was in power mode. Still sexy, but very in charge. More of the "I'm doing fine on my own" message. Ray still wasn't sure what Wanetta saw in him. But she'd agreed to take him seriously if he could get along with Tiesha. And he wanted to be more than a boy-toy.

When Tiesha came back down the stairs, she looked dressed for carnival cruising. Jeans and a hoodie, sparkling sneakers, matching purse. Stylish for age ten. She got it from her momma. She gave her mother a hug, and Ray got a glare as he stood up. It beat a waving knife, so it would have to do.

They took Ray's Honda. It was actually roomier than Wanetta's car. He would have taken Wanetta for the SUV type, but apparently, she wasn't a mommy chauffeur. His ex-wife drove an SUV that Ray had paid for and tended to take Tyriq and his friends everywhere. Ray constantly thought of the contrasts. Meredith was the pampered poodle type. It had been what he wanted sixteen years ago. Long sleek hair, stiletto heels, and the anorexic look of a cover girl model. The only thing she had in common with Wanetta was a willingness to go out with him. Ray hadn't known what she'd seen in him either. But they had fallen into bed together, Meredith had gotten pregnant, and Ray tried doing the right thing. It had been a disaster from the beginning. Her parents hated him. Her friends shunned him or cooed around him like he was fresh meat. Meredith constantly harped on him to make more money. So, he sold cars. Luxury cars. At a Lexus dealership. He worked his mojo, hooked his customers, took in the money… and gave it to Meredith. But it was never enough. She left him for his boss, who promised her marriage but didn't follow through. Ray got downgraded to selling Acura's at another dealership. And still gave more than half of his salary to Meredith.

Wanetta had come in looking for an Acura. And oddly enough, he didn't sell her one. She ended up with a used Mercedes convertible. And he ended up with a girlfriend. It had been an odd thing. She had been ready to sign the contract but wanted to look around more. A few weeks later, she had driven up in the Mercedes and came by to apologize. He had asked her out then. A date at Applebee's, another at Outback, and eventually, after five months, a home-cooked meal and a taste of her own secret garden. They had dated every other weekend when Tiesha was with her father. They'd grown up on the same music, gone to rival high schools, and still lived separate lives. Sometimes, Ray wondered if Wanetta knew Meredith. Stranger things had happened.

The carnival was packed with youngsters screaming, whining, cajoling, and dragging their parents around. The older ones with no parents hung in bunches, crowding the younger kids out of the way to get at the games and rides. But the screams were the same. Carnival rides seemed to have that effect on everyone. Even parents screamed - the ones that dared to get on the rides. It seemed you couldn't keep it in, no matter how old you were. Ray thought it was the rickety quality of the rides. That adult knowledge that maybe the ride was too old, and the metal struts wouldn't hold up. The drop of the rollercoaster felt as though something had broken, and the scream just escaped from your throat. Ray wanted to convince Wanetta and Tiesha to go on something more benign, but Tiesha wasn't having it, and Wanetta gave him a look that said, "Sissy, man up." So, they got in the line for the biggest, scariest, most rickety looking rollercoaster at the carnival. It took forever, standing there with Wanetta, avoiding adult conversation, listening to Tiesha people-watching, pointing out the kids she knew, and discussing exactly what she knew about them with her mother. The conversation was frighteningly teen-aged for a ten-year-old. Even at 15, Tyriq had no interest in girls at all. Tiesha was dissecting each boy, his clothes, his hair, and his potential as boyfriend material. She waved at some of them if she deemed them worthy. Ray took it in in amazement. He would never have guessed that women appraised men in the same way that men appraised women. Although the body parts being appraised were a bit different. It made sense in a way. At age ten, you weren't thinking about a guy's earning potential. That came later.

It was during Ray's musings that he caught sight of Meredith. He felt his penis shrivel up the way it had when Tiesha had brandished her carving knife at him. Any semblance of love he had ever felt for her had been replaced by a loathing that he only barely stifled when Tyriq was around. That loathing he felt with every child support check he signed. He knew from Tyriq that Meredith was constantly bringing men home, and there was nothing he could do about it. He'd married a whore; he just hadn't figured it out at the time.

Ray was at the top of the line and found himself jumping onto the rollercoaster with an embarrassing eagerness, as though it would fly him away from the mess he knew was coming. And at that moment, she looked up for some unknown reason. And Ray felt his life change. If Wanetta had never known Meredith before, they were going to meet in the next five minutes, and there was nothing he could do about it.

She was standing waiting for them at the exit line. Cornering them like a female hyena, with Ray as a potential kill. But there was no purr. "So, who's the black b----, Ray?" Meredith flicked her blonde hair out of her eyes and smiled.

It was like a stab in the gut from which he was not going to recover. He shouldn't have needed to defend himself, but the feeling was there. So, he did the only thing he could do and took the offensive. "Wanetta, meet my ex-wife, Meredith. Meredith, meet my future wife, Wanetta." It wasn't really a lie. It was a hope, a message, a throwing down of the gauntlet. A challenge he shouldn't have to make but did so anyway. He could be civil, and in being civil, make Meredith look like a witch. Meredith responded. "So, the black b---- is your fiancée?" Isn't that cute?" The man in Ray wanted to punch Meredith in the face. Why wasn't it legal? They were fighting words. "Actually, I consider her several steps up" Ray tried to step forward. Tried to end it. But he hadn't counted on Tiesha. "So, you were married to her?" "And now you expect to marry MY mom. I don't think so."

Tiesha had moved between Ray and Wanetta, pushing Ray closer to Meredith.

"Oh, this must be mini-b----. Too cute. And I guess the marriage thing isn't happening, and this is just some whore you picked up off the street." Ray slapped Meredith before he could think. In front of a crowd of people. Most of whom had probably not heard the conversation but only saw a black man hit a white woman. A crowd sprung up around him. A white man reached to pull up Meredith, who had conveniently fallen on the ground like some damsel in distress. Another white man punched Ray in the gut. As he was falling, what cut Ray to the quick was seeing Tyriq. Knowing that Tyriq had seen Ray hit his mother. And there was no way to erase that image from his son's eyes. So, he was not surprised when Tyriq looked at him with disgust and disapproval. Tyriq would defend his mother, not knowing what she had said or why Ray had slapped her. Ray stayed down. Maybe on the ground was safer. Maybe not defending himself would end it. A lot of maybes. It worked, though. The crowd dispersed when it was clear there would be no fight. Meredith had gone, presumably with the man who helped her up. And the only two people standing over him were Wanetta and Tiesha.

He was surprised they had stayed. Wanetta gave him a hand up. "She had it coming." But Tiesha was crying. Within five minutes, he had seen two children hurt, and there was so little he could do about it.

"I want to go home." The day was ruined. His chance to win over Tiesha was ruined. All because of a mistake he made sixteen years ago that would haunt him for life.

They headed for the car in silence, except for Tiesha's sniffles. Wanetta held Tiesha's hand. Ray stood a little apart from her. Giving her space, giving them space. When they got to the car, Wanetta got into the back seat with Tiesha, and Ray knew things were over. When they got to Wanetta's house, there was no "I'll call you." Just a very firm "Goodbye, Ray." Unforgiven.

Ray drove home in alternating emotions of rage and dejection. As he pulled into the driveway, his phone rang. It was Wanetta. "I just got Tiesha settled down. I just wanted to tell you I know that woman provoked you, but what you did went too far. If you could hit her, you could hit me, and I'm not going to let that kind of man be in my life."

Ray pulled back out of the driveway and headed to Meredith's. What used to be Their house. He saw her Lexus SUV in the driveway. He walked up to the front door and rang the bell. She answered it with a black mark on the side of her face he knew he had put there. He felt only minor regret.

"Why. What right did you have to tear down my life? You sad little witch. Your life is so bad that you have to ruin mine." He wished he feared that Tyriq would hear him, but he had already lost Tyriq, just as he had lost Wanetta.

"You didn't deserve her. And I was just letting her know."

Ray stepped inside the house this time. Nobody needed to see. He punched Meredith in the face, and it was satisfying. When she went down, there would be no one to save her. Ray picked her up and punched her again. He saw blood spurt from her nose. He hoped he had broken it. Meredith was screaming. Ray socked her in the gut. She caved. She whimpered.

All of those years, all of those memories, all of the madness. It just rose up. At this moment, did anything really need to be said? Ray reached for Meredith's throat, brought her up to eye-level, and said, "You white trash whore. I wish you were dead."

As if to make Ray's wish come true, the bullet from the 9-mm gun that Ray had taught Tyriq to shoot went through his back, through his heart, out the other side, and lodged into Meredith's right lung. They both sank to the floor. The last thing Ray heard was Tyriq crying for his mother.

Around the Table

"So, how soon is too soon?"

D'Jaris was sitting around the kitchen table with the Chocolate Drops: Ryan – stylish and sensible with a crown of braids, Renee – short, natural-haired, and matter-of-fact, Kim – busty, pony-tailed and always devout, and Keisha – slim and feisty with long blond locks and a small nose ring. They were her sister-friends since high school 40 years ago, line sisters with Zeta Phi Beta, and always there for each other: from Keisha's abortion to D'Jaris' divorce, to Renee's breast cancer, to the suicide of Kim's son. Tonight, they were sipping after-dinner Baileys and discussing the serious question. Renee was the first to speak.

"Chile, be real. You've only had one date. Do you think Mr. Right just landed in your lap? And Keisha, say nothing."

"Why are you on me?" said Keisha, rolling her eyes.

"Because you never wait more than twenty-four hours, and you always, always get hurt," said Renee, as she pointed her finger at Keisha.

"No, not always," scoffed Keisha. "There have been a few who were so lame in bed that I couldn't get attached if they came up with a diamond ring."

"Keisha has a point," said Ryan, waving her glass. "You don't want to wait so long that you're catching feelings, and then you find out he doesn't have the goods."

"Now wait," said Kim shaking her head, "not being Mr. Right in bed does not automatically disqualify a man."

"So, Kim, what you sayin' about Tony?" said Renee, eyebrows raised.

"Don't disrespect my husband. He just needed some teachin'," declared Kim. "He's fine now. At any rate, D'Jaris, you gotta wait. As Renee said, you've only had one date, and you can't really go by what Keisha says unless you want a life of one-night stands."

"There have been some major good nights in those stands, and I've had a few that lasted up to a year," said Keisha, pouting.

"And then what happened?" "You dumped them because you wanted more than sex, and that was all they had to offer," stated Renee.

"Keisha," said Ryan, in her patient voice, "try switching it up. Make sure he has it upstairs before you check with downstairs."

"This is about D'Jaris tonight," snapped Keisha. "Not me. So, spill D'Jaris. What's he like."

D'Jaris paused to sip her Bailey's. "Well, he's white," she said hesitantly.

"Hold up!" cried a quartet of voices.

"That's it. He has to wait." Said Keisha. Everybody nodded.

"He's got a lot to prove," said Renee. "You've got to know, really know, that he's worth spreading your legs for. He could be sniffing around for overseer sex."

"But what if all I want is sex?" said D'Jaris, coyly playing devil's advocate.

"Don't lie, D'Jaris," Ryan rejoined. "You wouldn't have asked the question if you didn't care. And he must have done something right if you're sitting up with us, asking the question."

"So, spill," said Kim, leaning forward. "What did he do that was sooooooooo right?"

"And what's his name?" piped up Keisha.

"His name is Harvey Branson."

"Noooooo! Not Harvey!" Ryan recoiled playfully.

"Yeah, Harvey. Get over it already," said D'Jaris, glaring at Ryan. "He took me to Ruth's Chris."

"Five star restaurant. Alright, I'm over it. Go on," gushed Ryan.

"He prayed over dinner," sighed D'Jaris.

"Wow!" Kim exclaimed, raising her glass to D'Jaris as a cheer. "That says a lot. I think I'm over him being white!"

"It gets better," added D'Jaris. "He showed me pictures of his family. His stepfather is black. His little sister is mixed. Harvey talked about how he and his stepfather screen her boyfriends. His biological father ditched his mother when he was two. His biological father's name was also Harvey, but Branson is Harvey's stepfather's name."

"Yeah," said Keisha, nodding approval, "he can be white. That's some deep shit."

"OK," said Renee, taking a sip. "What else?"

"I'll show you a selfie we took," said D'Jaris, playfully, "but you gotta be chill because he's nothing to look at."

"We'll judge," said Ryan, matter-of-factly.

"Um, D'Jaris?" said Keisha as the cellphone went around. "He looks like a white Urkel. He's got the big glasses, a bony face, receding gray hair, and a big nose. Sheesh."

"I said 'Be Chill,'" said D'Jaris harshly. "I already said he doesn't have it in the looks department."

"Then why, oh why, are you even remotely thinking about sleeping with him," said Keisha, grinning.

"I understand," said Kim soothingly. "Y'all said the same thing about Tony. Glasses, overweight, pigeon-toed, and you know, it made me wait. But the man worked to get some real action. Worked himself right into a marriage. And it has been a really good thing."

"Yes, yes, Kim, we all know how happy you are," Keisha snapped. "This is about D'Jaris."

"To be honest, when I met him," D'Jaris explained, "I immediately thought of Kim and Tony. I think that's why I wanted to give him a chance, not judge on the exterior package."

"And Ruth's Chris," exclaimed Ryan. "Let's not forget Ruth's Chris."

"I've got to confess; I'm not feeling any need to jump into bed with him. With the white Urkel thing and all. But do you know," said D'Jaris, glowing, "All he did all night was tell me that he thought I was beautiful. He says he likes to look into my eyes; my lips look kissable, and my skin reminds him of a Lindt Truffle. When I think about how many bruthas dis me because I'm too dark for them, this really pulled me up."

"You are beautiful, D'Jaris," said Kim smiling. "We've been telling you that for years."

"Um, duh," D'Jaris pointed out, "it's different coming from a guy. More than once. And with intense eyes."

"Now he's sounding like a stalker," Renee cringed.

"Did I mention that he pulled back the chair and held the door?" asked D'Jaris.

"Still could be a stalker," mumbled Ryan.

"OK, here's the clue that he's not a stalker," D'Jaris responded. "He's going to wait for my call. Any time. My move."

"That's different," stated Keisha.

"I think it's because he knows he's Urkel. He wants to be wanted. Can't blame him for that," quipped Renee, taking a sip.

"And would you believe he went to an HBCU?" mentioned D'Jaris.

"Seriously?" asked Kim.

"He went to Fisk," said D'Jaris, nodding her head. "It was his stepfather's alma mater. I think he got a legacy scholarship. Can't pass up the money!"

"So, he's a mix," Ryan counted off on her fingers. "White Urkel, Ruth's Chris, prays before dinner, chivalrous, black stepfather, baby sister that he protects. What else ya got?"

"Would you believe, not much else because he wanted to hear about me," said D'Jaris, smiling again.

"Now that's a keeper," said Keisha, twirling her locks. "A man who can listen. Doesn't come along every day. Maybe you could marry him and have a piece on the side."

"KEISHA!" exclaimed Kim.

"I'm just joking," Keisha grinned.

Well, now I know why you're asking the question," said Ryan pensively. "It's got to be thought about."

"Now wait, are you saying that if he was a fine black brother, the answer would be different?" said Keisha, giving Ryan a raised eyebrow.

"Not exactly; it depends on what you want," explained Renee. "If you just want to hit it, you don't wait. If he acts into himself, you don't wait because you know it won't last. If he acts into you, then you do a 'Think Like a Man' trip and wait for him to call you his girlfriend or to say he loves you. And then you just get caught up in the moment."

"Back to Harvey," sighed D'Jaris. "What about him?"

Keisha raised an empty glass, and D'Jaris got up to get her a refill. She topped off Ryan and Renee's glasses as well, then put the bottle of Bailey's back on the counter and sat down again.

"Sometime between 'I love you' and 'Will You Marry Me,'"

"Definitely not before 'I love you'," added Renee.

"He could be the jewelry buying type," Ryan piped up. "I say jewelry plus 'I love you'."

"And you have to meet his mother," said Renee fiercely.

"Yeah," nodded Keisha, "that's serious."

"OK," said D'Jaris, holding up 3 fingers, "jewelry, I love you, meet his mother."

"Hold up. What if he rushes things? All of this could happen in the first month. We gotta put some time on this," Ryan pointed out.

"Six months," declared Kim.

"That seems kind of extreme," said D'Jaris, frowning.

"I waited until Tony and I were engaged. And he took a year to propose," explained Kim.

"Oh Kim, no, you didn't," gasped Renee, tilting her head.

"Yep, don't think I didn't eat the banana a few times, but he waited for the good stuff," explained Kim. "Waiting is important."

"How long did you wait, Ryan?" asked D'Jaris.

"Well, um, not that long," Ryan smiled, remembering. "Frank was so shy; I had to jump him. So, it was actually 2 months. But he had definitely said "I love you" and he gave me little stud diamond earrings. His mother's in Oregon, so that had to wait."

"Whatever you do, don't jump him, D'Jaris," said Kim, shaking her head, ponytail flipping.

"I don't know about that. If he's letting her make the moves, then I think she gets to pick the time. But definitely at least 2 months, and maybe 3," argued Renee.

"One other thing. We get to meet him first," declared Ryan.

"That's true. He has to get the Chocolate Drops seal of approval," Keisha nodded.

"And meet his friends, too," suggested Renee. "That's another requirement. Are you adding them up? 'I love you', jewelry, meet his mother, meet his friends, he meets us, 2-3 months."

"I think I got it," D'Jaris announced. "I think I'm going to call him tonight and set up that second date. It's been three days. He's waited long enough. I just wanted to talk to y'all first. Thanks for coming out so quickly."

"D'Jaris, you cook like a dream," sighed Keisha. "You can always get us to come over."

"I love you guys," said D'Jaris, wistfully. "You are the sisters I never had."

"We are your sisters. Never forget it," declared Keisha.

"I won't," D'Jaris smiled. "Cheesecake for dessert. I made it last night." D'Jaris stood, went to the fridge, pulled out a large cheesecake topped with cherries, and placed it on the table. She then went and got 5 plates and spoons and a cake knife. As she filled the plates, the Chocolate Drops passed them around. A reward for a question answered, a problem solved.

Acknowledgments

This collection of short stories has been in the making for nearly 15 years and would not have happened except for the fact that I was able to share individual stories with my friends, and they told me to publish. So, I thank Kristy McKinnon, Arzoo Wasson, Karen Braithwaite Yarn, Harriette Matthews and especially Jody Zolli for believing that my stories belonged in print.

The second group of people who made a major difference in the quality of my stories were the people who reviewed my work at www.TheNextBigWriter.com, from 2010 forward. This includes Marilyn Johnson, Ann Everett, "7sistersseen" and many others who offered re-writes, edits, and suggestions, but who also told me that my stories were good and enjoyable to read.

One person in particular made an enormous difference in my work. In 2019, Michelle Tawmging offered to professionally do a deep dive on my stories. What she did was phenomenal. She got into the stories, she got into the characters, she pointed out where she didn't have enough information. She pointed to characters she thought were unsympathetic, she looked to see if the story came full circle and answered all of the important questions. Her critique was worth every penny, and I will always be in her debt.

My project manager at Excel Book Writing, Racheal Thomas, also deserves special mention. Racheal put up with me, my harsh critiques of the artwork, my unsolicited ideas about marketing, my temper tantrums, and my pushy questions, and my insistence that the project move along as fast as possible, for the entire time that the book was with the publishers. She gets major kudos, as does the entire project team at Excel Book Writing.

I thank my ARC Team: Tylia Simpson, Joan Motz, Lauren N. Morris, Destiny Rawls, Dosha Ellis Beard, Shawn L. Williams, Shanese Harley, Chrissy Walker-Allen, Dennis White, Marla Richardson, Lorna Sgammato, Aprel Barnes, Bill Dixon, Kara Kuykendall, Delores Logan. Peg Lou, Marilyn Johnson and especially Margaret Lark Russell. These wonderful people saw my description of the book, often without knowing me at all, decided that they wanted to read it, and were willing to post a review on Amazon. Because of them, I was able to move the book forward on a host of platforms that wanted GOOD books, with four stars or more. My ARC Team wrote the reviews that propelled me forward, and I am forever grateful.

Last but never least, I thank the fifty members of my Facebook support group. Even though I have not named you all, please know that you are very, very special to me. Since I began this project, you have put up with me, encouraged me, helped me with ideas, given necessary critiques with my graphics and descriptions, told me when story ideas and descriptions were inappropriate, offered resources and connections, and helped me get through this roller coaster ride. For the past three years, and often longer, you have been my support system, getting me through all manner of things, this publishing process included. Thank you for being there for me, always, in all ways.

Social media handles

Twitter:

https://twitter.com/BougieAfro

Instagram:

https://www.instagram.com/afrobougieblues/

What did you think of Afro-Bougie Blues?

First of all, thank you for purchasing this book, ***Afro-Bougie Blues.*** *I know you could have picked any number of books to read, but you picked this book and for that I am extremely grateful.*

I hope it was an enjoyable read for you. If so, it would be really nice if you could share this book with your friends and family by posting to Facebook and Twitter.

I'd also like to hear from you and hope that you could take some time to post a review on-line. I want you, the reader, to know that your review is very important. Your feedback and support will help me to greatly improve my writing craft for future projects and make this book even better.

I thank you and wish you all the best!

- Lauren Wilson

Made in the USA
Columbia, SC
13 January 2023

10240045R00093